D0209917

BOOK 5

THE WORLD'S FAIR

T. L. TEDROW

SCHOLASTIC INC.
New York Toronto London Auckland Sydney

ISBN 0-590-22656-8

Copyright © 1992 by Thomas L. Tedrow. Illustrations by Dennas Davis. All rights reserved. Published by Scholastic Inc., 555 Broadway, New York, NY 10012, by arrangement with Thomas Nelson Publishing.

12 11 10 9 8 7 6 5 4 3 2 1   5 6 7 8 9/9 0/0

Printed in the U.S.A.   40

First Scholastic printing, January 1995

To my pretty wife Carla and our younguns,
C.T., Tyler, Tara and Travis.

May we never forget the magic of childhood dreams which
is really what being young at heart is all about.

And to my good friends at Thomas Nelson,
for making these dreams come true.

CONTENTS

FOREWORD

Laura Ingalls Wilder is loved the world over for her pioneer books and the wonderful television series that was based on them. Though much has been written about the Old West, it was Laura Ingalls Wilder who brought the frontier to life for millions of young readers.

The Laura Ingalls Wilder story did not stop after her last book. She and her husband, Manly, and daughter, Rose, moved to Mansfield, Missouri, from South Dakota in 1894. Laura was twenty-seven, Manly thirty-eight, and Rose was seven. They arrived with only one hundred dollars and the few possessions salvaged from their house that had burned.

They used the money as a down-payment on a broken down farm and after a decade of hard work, they had built Apple Hill Farm, the finest house Laura had ever lived in!

Laura Ingalls Wilder went on to become a pioneer journalist in Mansfield, where for sixteen years she wrote for a farm family weekly. She spoke her mind about the environment and land abuse, preached women's rights, lamented the consequences of war, and observed the march of progress as cars, planes, radios, and new inventions changed America forever.

America was proud of itself. In the first decade of this century, five World's Fairs were held for America to showcase its accomplishments. Thousands of people flocked to see the gaudy and wonderous exhibits: strange-looking motor cars, airships, and electrical gadgets such as the *automatic dishwasher*. What today is the commonplace was, at the turn of the century, wonderful and futuristic.

One of these remarkable World's Fairs was held in St. Louis, and all America was singing the song "Meet Me in St. Louis, Louis." It was a happy, wonderful linking element that brought our ethnically diverse nation together in spirit and harmony.

As an adjunct to the Fair, the Third Olympic Games were staged to take advantage of the crowds coming to St. Louis. In *The World's Fair,* book five of "The Days of Laura Ingalls Wilder," Laura covers the event for her newspaper, *The Mansfield Monitor*. As part of her assignment, she takes in the Olympics and an athletic "freak" show called, "Anthropology Days." Based on actual events, what Laura witnesses is so disturbing that she is forced to take action.

While this book is a fictional account of Laura's life, it retains the historical integrity of her columns, diary, family background, personal beliefs, and the general history of the times in which she lived. However, any references to specific events, real people, or real places are intended only to give the fiction a setting in historical reality. Names, characters, and incidents are either the product of the author's imagination or are used fictitiously, and their resemblance, if any, to real-life counterparts is purely coincidental.

T. L. Tedrow

CHAPTER 1

OZARK SPRING

Spring had come to the Ozarks. The hills were clothed in every shade of new-life green imaginable, stitched with the bright colors of buds and blossoms sprouting along the creek-beds and roadsides.

The sounds of new life and new beginnings were in the air day and night. From the first crow of the morning rooster to the cricket symphonies that put the mountains and hollows to sleep, the spring of 1906 hinted at the promise of good summer crops and full fall harvests.

Laura stood on the front porch of Apple Hill Farm and looked out over the northern lights that danced over the Ozark heavens. She sat in the porch swing, mesmerized, watching the magnificent display.

It was the second time in six months that the night skies had come ablaze in color. The rippling waves of bluish-green that spread across the sky were like hanging draperies, flapping on the edge of nature's night.

Manly came out and stood beside his wife of half a lifetime. He placed his hand lightly on her shoulder, feeling the warmth that came over his soul every time he touched her.

"What causes them things?" he asked, looking toward the northern lights.

Laura took his hand and carefully turned his wedding band in a slow circle. "No one really knows. Hill people say it's spirits dancing and *National Geographic* magazine said it might be sunlight reflecting off polar ice packs."

Seventeen-year-old Rose, home for spring break from the private school she attended in New Orleans, came out and stood beside her father. "In school I read how in ancient times, the Roman King Tiberius Caeser saw a deep red aurora and thought it was a gigantic fire in the outlying colonies. So he sent a legion of soldiers to put it out."

"What do you think it is?" Manly asked Laura. "Ghosts dancin'?"

Laura shrugged her shoulders and smiled. "I just think that whatever it is, it's sure beautiful." Manly nodded and went back into the house.

Laura and Rose stood still, peering into the night sky. The evening's silence was broken only by the crickets chirping their good-bye to winter. Rose cocked her ear to their sounds.

"They taught me in school that if you count the number of cricket chirps in 15 seconds and add 37, you will know what the temperature is."

"Just don't tell that to your father," Laura said with a laugh. "He'd spend the rest of the night trying to get the count right." Rose chuckled and Laura took the opportunity to turn the conversation to Rose's school. "You love your school in New Orleans, don't you?"

The answer was obvious in Rose's eyes. "The school is wonderful. I . . . I can't thank you and Daddy enough for everything you've sacrificed." In a sudden burst of emotion, Rose rested her head on her mother's shoulder as if she were a little girl again.

Manly came back out onto the porch and smiled with pleasure when he saw the mother and daughter so enjoying each other's company.

He quietly walked over to where they were standing and put his arms around them both. "You've got more education than your Ma and me combined. But everytime somethin' smart like that bit of history comes out of your mouth, I know it's worth every penny we scraped together to send you there."

A chorus of night birds sang their approval.

CHAPTER 2

ATTIC MEMORIES

After the kitchen was cleaned and Manly and Rose had turned in for the night, Laura remembered something she couldn't place. There was something about the northern lights that made her think of another night long ago.

She remembered being asleep in the back of Pa's wagon. Just a little girl clutching her doll, protected from the evils of the world by her parents. Her dog was nestled beside her, and overhead, shooting stars skated across the skies as if part of a grand stage show. Laura remembered falling asleep, thinking the world was awash in Christmas colors.

It was somewhere in Kansas, but she couldn't remember exactly where or when. Maybe it would be in one of her diaries, bundled in her memory trunk in the attic. Stepping carefully up the narrow stairs, she navigated through the boxes of things too important to throw away but not important enough to ever use again. *I guess I'm a packrat,* she thought, looking around.

The single bulb hanging from the ceiling cast strange shadows against the rafters and pointed nails overhead. Laura found her memory trunk under a cloth in the corner. She pulled up the old oak rocker with a cracked rib and sat down.

She carefully unhooked the brass clasps and lifted the lid. The hinges creaked, the dust swirled in the beam of light, and a flood of memories came rushing back.

She thought about how she saved things to remember moments she wanted to touch again. How the physical objects brought back the taste, touch, and feel of a moment in time long past. *The mind is a miracle,* she thought.

Laura picked up the first rag doll that she carried across the prairie. Most people would think it a sad bundle of cloth, tied and sewn together with button eyes. But to Laura, it was better than any store-bought doll.

She held the doll to her chest and closed her eyes, thinking of the nights when wolves howled outside their door and Indian drum beats pierced the darkness on those lonely prairies. How she lay there trusting her parents to protect her, but thinking that *she* was the one protecting her dolly.

There were no soldiers to call for help because Laura and her family were miles from nowhere. Just Pa with his rifle and Ma with her knitting, rocking by the fire. Both tried to look calm so as not to scare the children, but both were afraid that the wolves would kill the sheep or the Indians would attack.

Digging further in the trunk, she found a family picture with Shep, their big St. Bernard dog. Everyone was dressed in their Sunday finest, looking formal and stiff. Everyone except Pa. No matter how hard he tried to look like a father was supposed to look, he always had a gleam in his eye that even the camera caught!

Laura was startled. She thought she heard Pa's voice calling out, "Where's my little half-pint of sweet cider half drunk up?"

She looked around, wide-eyed with confusion. *No, I didn't*

hear anything except the strings of my heart telling me it's time to go visit Ma and Pa. They're getting old.

Pa's visit in February had finally convinced her that he, too, would pass away. *Excuses not to see your aging parents are only good until they slap you in the face at their funeral,* she thought. *Then you have to carry the regrets of your selfishness to the grave.*

"I'm going to go see Ma and Pa in the summer," Laura said to the shadows surrounding her.

A slight breeze outside the attic window tinkled the windchimes on the porch, reminding her to keep this promise. It was a message of urgency that dimmed the dangling bulb and seemed to shroud her in darkness.

"Must be trouble with the lines," she whispered, trying to reassure herself as people do when suddenly cast into darkness.

As the light brightened again, she saw a bouquet of dried flowers, which broke her melancholy mood. She smiled at the memory they brought back. Laura could remember the day she collected them as if it were just the day before.

The flowers were attached to her diary of that year. It was like stepping back in time, as she turned each page, looking at the handwriting of the little girl she once was. So full of hopes, dreams, and emotions; untutored, but wise beyond her years:

> *Someone broke the window at the school today. The pieces of glass were scattered across the ground. Some of the girls had picked Sweet William flowers and were looking at the broken window.*
>
> *Jenny stuck a wet petal against a piece of broken glass. Then another and another. Soon she had a beautiful arrangement when you looked from the other side. We all*

tried it, holding them up to the sun to dry. It was as if you had a looking glass into life itself in your hands!
   I will save these forever to remind me of how wonderful life is.

Her diaries were in order by year, so she looked through the stack of nickel note pads and found her writings from the territories. *If my memory serves me well,* she thought, *the northern lights happened after we left our prairie house.*
She looked through those diary years, skipping pages as if they were but seconds in time—pages that represented the labored writings of a home-taught girl.
Laura found herself thinking it was like going to the nickelodeon movies. Time that once moved so slowly in a little girl's mind was flying with each page turned, like the new airships that she'd read about.
Finally, in the diary about moving to Plum Creek, Laura found it:

   Tonight I could hardly sleep. The sky was on fire! Pa said it was angels dancing when God wasn't looking, but Ma told me he was only teasing. It seemed as if rainbows were being shook out like sheets across the heavens. Like a colorful picnic blanket for the stars to rest on had been laid down. The shooting stars played hide-and-go-seek, crossing the heavens like Fourth of July fireworks. It was a glorious night.

Laura had found what she was looking for, but still in the trunk in front of her were memories ranging from her early childhood to the birth of her daughter. She rooted through the memory trunk, pushing aside letters from friends and her first pair of shoes, and there Laura found Manly's love letters.
She couldn't help but smile as she opened the first one and

saw the careful hand of a boy-man not used to writing and not at all comfortable with the written word. But when those letters came on those lonely nights when she was a sixteen-year-old teacher, living away from home, they seemed to stretch her heartstrings across the prairie and tie them in a love knot with Manly's wherever he was at the moment.

Each letter was precious. About some matter that seemed so urgent at the time, something that only a teenage girl could understand. She remembered where she was when she received each one and the rush of emotions that had overcome her as she read them over and over.

A little memory of something they did. A private joke between them. Tidbits of gossip they shared. Two people trying to cross the strange and wondrous sea of emotions to bond together for life.

Near the end of the stack, she found a letter that stood out in her mind. It was one of his famous "promises" letters. He'd written her several in a row, promising things he would do if she would marry him. Laura ran her fingers through the letters isolating the promises made.

I promise to build us a successful farm or take a city job . . . I promise to build us the finest house in DeSmet, North Dakota . . . I promise to never move you again . . . I promise to . . .

Sitting back in the old rocker, Laura didn't notice the dust of time floating around her. She shrugged and said out loud "Manly, you sure never kept those promises."

"Who you talkin' to up here, woman?" Manly asked, bringing her back to the present. He was standing on the steps in his long nightshirt, looking like an overgrown boy.

"Oh, Manly, I'm just—"

"I know, every time you come up here you don't get anything done 'cause you spend all your time thinkin' about the past."

Laura sighed. "The northern lights reminded me about a night on the prairie long ago. I just wanted to see if it was in one of my diaries."

"Did you find it?"

She nodded. "It was in the Plum Creek diary. I guess I just got lost in thought."

"Well, don't stay up all night," he said, heading back down the stairs. "Hope you won't be too tired to make me breakfast. I'm goin' to be powerful hungry."

Manly started back down the stairs. Laura looked at the love letters in her hand and called after him. "Manly, I found your love letters. Remember those?"

She heard him stop and walk carefully back up the stairs until his face peeked over the edge. She continued, "Yup, I found your famous list of promises and—"

Manly took a few more steps. "Now, Laura, those were written a long time ago, and—"

"Want to hear them?"

"No. I just want to get to sleep."

"Yes sir, you promised me that—hold on, let me read some of them to you." Manly groaned as she shuffled through the letters. "Listen to this one. 'I promise our first farm will be successful or I'll take the city job and live like you want me to.' " She looked at Manly and shook her head. "And this: 'I promise to learn to play the piano.' " Laura read it again, just to be sure. *"Play the piano?* Really, Manly, what possessed you to write such a silly thing."

"You wanted to *marry a man with culture,"* he said in a mocking tone. "So I thought I could learn to play the pi-an-nee but the darn thing's got too many keys."

Laura laughed. "Manly Wilder! We've had a piano downstairs for years and I've never heard you even try to play 'Chopsticks.' "

Manly started back down the stairs. "And you never will. It's time to go to bed. Come on, it's late."

Laura looked down at the last love letter in the stack and blinked. She had forgotten this one—the one that had gotten her hook, line, and sinker.

"Manly," she called after him, "listen to this whopper of all whoppers."

Manly groaned from the bottom of the stairs. "This is the last one."

"Manly, you promised me that . . ." She paused for effect but felt the memory of this unfulfilled promise seeping into her.

Manly rolled his eyes. He could tell by the tone of her voice that she had opened up the old hornet's nest. He'd hoped *this* promise had been forgotten with time.

". . . you promised me that if I married you, you would take me on a big-city honeymoon." Laura stopped. She stared at the letter in her hand, thinking about the honeymoon she'd never had.

Manly leaned against the stairwell wall, knowing that life on Apple Hill would change for the worst for the next few days until it blew over again. *That durn promise is like the locusts and grasshoppers that bury themselves to come out and haunt you year after year.*

"Laura, honey, I told you that one day we'll go on that honeymoon. Anytime you want to girl, why, we'll pack up and go stay the night at the Mansfield Hotel."

Laura looked toward the voice as if she was hearing someone speak in a foreign language. She stood up and walked over to the stairwell. Staring down on Manly she said, "Stay the night at the Mansfield Hotel? You call that a big-city honeymoon? We *live* in Mansfield, you goose egg."

Manly had a sheepish grin on his face. As she looked at him standing there in his silly-looking nightshirt, Laura wanted to be mad, but couldn't. No matter how hard she tried, all she wanted to do was laugh and hug him.

"Laura, I'll take you anywhere we can afford. Heck, even a few miles farther to where we can't afford. Whatever will make you happy, girl. That's all I want."

"Go to sleep, Manly. I just want to sit and think for a while."

"Come on to bed, honey."

"I'll be down in a while. Everything's okay."

Manly shrugged and stepped off the last stair. As the attic door closed, Laura walked back over and sat in the rocker under the flickering bulb. She picked up her dolly and held it on her lap.

I shouldn't have gotten upset. But I dreamed for a big wedding and a honeymoon. I wish Manly was more romantic and would take me on a honeymoon. That would be wonderful.

"I'll make sure Rose doesn't miss out," she said to the dust in the air. "Rose will have her long white dress and big wedding day."

Laura clutched her old dolly and turned off the light. She rocked slowly back and forth, thinking about prayers, promises, dreams, and life's realities.

She nodded off, sleeping the night in the attic, surrounded by her memories and holding her dolly, protecting it once again against the world outside.

CHAPTER 3

A PROMISE TO BE KEPT

When Manly awakened Laura the next morning, her neck was stiff and her back ached from the curve in the rocker. She tried stretching on the porch and taking a short walk, but she still felt rusty. Even the sounds of spring in the air didn't make her feel any better.

"You could have come to the attic to wake me up," she said, holding her neck at the kitchen table.

"I did come back up, but you were sittin' there all hypnotized-like, lookin' at your old dolly," he said.

Laura looked at him. "I was thinking about the big-city honeymoon you never took me on. Your promises are about as solid as Swiss cheese."

"Oh, Laura, that was long ago. You shouldn't carry anger, it will give you stomach disease."

Laura was irritated, but her neck hurt so bad, she couldn't think of anything else—except having another cup of coffee. She poured another cup and sat looking at the steaming brew, sweetened by a teaspoon of sugar. The cream swirled in a marbled pattern.

Manly poured his third cup and sat down to the breakfast of

biscuits and gravy Laura had struggled to make. After they finished eating, Manly smacked his lips over the meal. After watching Laura rub her neck, he poured some hot water on a cloth and placed it on her sore muscles. Laura smiled and closed her eyes, enjoying the warmth.

"I guess this means you won't be helpin' with the chores this morning," he said softly.

Laura opened one eye and shook her head. "Manly, between spreading hay and shoveling manure, I've always been there to help you. *I keep my promises.*"

It was a cutting, unkind remark that Laura immediately regretted. "I'm sorry. I shouldn't have said that."

"That's okay," Manly said, putting more hot water on the cloth. But his feelings had been hurt.

"No, I shouldn't be saying things like that. No sense worrying over a honeymoon when we've got so much to be thankful for."

Manly tried to make light of things and smiled. "I think you got yourself so worked up in the attic over one of my old love letters that you twisted your neck and couldn't move."

"Oh, Manly." Laura laughed and took his hand. "Go on now and get your chores done. I'll clean up the kitchen."

Manly grabbed up one of her *Good Housekeeping* magazines and headed off.

She started to get up, but sat back down, rubbing her neck. "Bring that back," she called after him. "Use the *Montgomery Ward* book or the old *Ladies Home Journal.* I cut the pages into quarters and left them on the bench."

"You gonna be 'round all day?" Manly asked, handing the magazine back to her.

"I've got to go to town and see if Summers has anything he wants me to write about."

Manly picked up the paper from the day before and pointed

to a full-page ad for the Mansfield Annual Dog Show. "Why don't you write about dogs. Everyone loves dogs."

Laura shrugged. "I don't make the assignments."

Manly left to do the chores while Laura struggled with each dish. She watched him limp to the barn door and realized that his leg hurt him every hour of the day. Her neck pain would go away but the pain from the stroke he'd suffered in the Dakotas would be there until his last day on earth.

"I love you, Manly Wilder," she said out loud in the kitchen. "You've always done your best."

Jack the dog yipped his approval as he headed out the door to be with Manly. Spring was in the air and farmers throughout Wright County were preparing to plant. There were fields to plow and orchards to clean. Equipment had to be inspected carefully and hired hands found. Animals needed cutting, fixing, and breeding.

Farm life was tough. Up at dawn and still working at dark. Manly and Laura had already prepared their garden and cleaned out the brush from the orchards. They had cleaned out the basement storage and culled through the last of the stored carrots, turnips, beets, potatoes, onions, and apples. "One rotten apple will spoil the whole bin," Manly would always say to Laura as they worked side by side.

Their cows had to be milked by hand, each cow into separate buckets. That was the only way you could tell how much milk each cow was giving. "You get to know each udder," Manly would tell Laura, which was why they each had their own sides of the cow to milk.

Now he had to work on Laura's side of the cow as well as his own, and he wasn't at all pleased. The slope-eyed guernsey stared back at him and mooed quietly. Manly pulled at her udders. "People always say that a cow gives milk. That's hogwash! You know it, girl?" he asked the cow. She turned and gave him a single moo in reply.

"It ain't easy to get milk," he said, moving around the udder. "It sure takes a lot of pullin'!"

He yanked down too hard. "Sorry, girl. Ain't used to Laura's side." Jack, their old bulldog, came up and sat beside him. "And what do you want, old boy?" he asked, scratching under the dog's chin. "You want some?"

Jack opened his mouth and Manly shot a stream of warm, fresh milk into the dog's mouth and all over his face. One of the barn cats came up and licked around on Jack until he growled and chased her up into the hayloft.

Even though they had money in the bank, Manly and Laura scrimped and saved on everything they could. Neither of them would ever forget those hard times on the prairie when they went without food to make payments to the bank.

The Wilders prided themselves on being self-sufficient. They put up their own vegetables and fruit in Mason jars, which lined the white-washed basement walls. They slaughtered their own chickens, pigs, and cattle, and only bought what they truly needed. It was only recently that Laura had quit making lye soap for laundry and dishes after she had learned how harsh it was to your skin.

After milking the cows and shoveling the manure, Manly headed for the house to say good-bye to Laura. But Laura was standing at the barn's entrance.

"I'm sorry for hurting your feelings this morning," she said sincerely.

"Shucks, girl, a body can't feel perfect every minute." Manly laughed in his good-natured way. "Even a good engine needs tuning sometimes." He walked over and rubbed Laura's neck. "How's the neck feel now?"

Laura closed her eyes, enjoying the neck rub. "That hot cloth you gave me helped and I did some stretching. It will be fine in an hour or so . . . just a little higher please," she said with a sigh. "I left a sandwich in the icebox for your lunch."

Manly stopped rubbing. "Only one?"

She patted his stomach. "You've been eating too many sweets and not doing enough chores. You'll thank me tonight for letting you do mine this morning."

"Just don't make a habit of it," he said, hitching up his pants. "You going to take the Olds or the buggy?"

"I think I'll take the Oldsmobile." She hugged him and walked off to the barn where the car was parked. Manly watched as she drove toward town, writing tablet at her side, until she was out of sight.

A duck honked overhead. Manly raised a make-believe shotgun and made a booming noise. Smiling to himself, he went behind the barn and leaned on the fence, looking out over the land.

"Being a farmer is a great life," he said to the animals around him.

Two cows mooed as if in agreement. Manly opened the gate and walked them toward the lower pasture. As he limped along, he looked at what he and Laura had done with the farm and thought of how blessed his life was. They had freedom, roots, and tranquility. Looking out over the rocky slopes, he knew they had it all.

Maybe he'd been following after tranquility all his life and didn't know it. He'd chased after the false dreams of riches, new wagons, and big cash crops, when all he had to do was take satisfaction in what he already had. In what he and Laura had built—Apple Hill Farm.

Manly took his hat off and admired the land. *Freedom, tranquility, faith in God, a good wife, a fine daughter, the farm.* Jack the dog yipped, and Manly patted him on the head. *And a trusted old dog. You couldn't ask for anything more out of life.*

Jack raced ahead yipping to the cows to walk faster. They

paid him no attention, but it was a friendly game the animals played every morning.

Manly smiled to himself. *Sure as the rocks on the slopes roll downhill, people get to know themselves without realizing it. It just comes with age.*

Manly was going on forty-eight years old and knew by the slowness of his step that, unlike the season around him, he was entering the autumn of his life. He could hear the rhythms beating inside, carrying him one heartbeat closer to that final day. Manly was glad he'd gotten to know himself early on in life and forgotten about the false goals that lead some men astray. He had everything that mattered.

Everything that mattered was his to have and his to love. He caught his breath thinking about Laura. *I love that woman with all my heart and soul. I'd give my life for her. I love you Laura.*

He stopped on the ridge and shouted out to the world, "Laura Wilder, you're going to have your honeymoon. This will be one promise that I'll keep before I die."

Birds chirped all around him. It was a wonderful morning to be alive!

CHAPTER 4

THE ASSIGNMENT

ndrew Jackson Summers, editor and publisher of *The Mansfield Monitor,* picked up the wall receiver of the ringing phone.

"Mansfield Monitor."

"Andy, is that you?" a voice crackled through the static on the line.

"Yes, this is Andrew. Who's calling?"

"Andy, you old windbag, this is Dunning!"

"Jack! Where you callin' from?" Summers asked, smiling broadly. His old friend Jack Dunning, who ran the city desk for the *St. Louis Post-Dispatch,* was one of the people with whom he'd broken into the newspaper business.

"St. Louis! Where you think? When you comin' up here?"

Summers was caught off guard. "Comin' up there? What's goin' on?"

"What's goin' on? The World's Fair, man, that's what's goin' on. And you should be coverin' it."

"I'd love to, but we don't have that kind of budget."

"You can stay at my place," Dunning said.

"I appreciate the offer, but I just can't get away."

"Look, Andy, I've got a favor owed me at a couple hotels 'round here. Why don't you catch the train up here and it'll be like old times again."

"Would the offer be good for one of my reporters?"

"What's his name?" Dunning asked wearily.

"It's a her. Laura Wilder."

"That's even better," Dunning said. "Is she pretty?"

"She's pretty married and quite happy."

"Rats." Dunning laughed through the static. "Can't blame me for hopin'."

Summers got all the details he needed and told Dunning he'd get back to him by the end of the day. *The World's Fair.* Summers grinned at the thought. *Just the assignment for Laura. I can't pay her what she's worth, so this will be a little surprise thank you.*

The song "Meet Me In St. Louis, Louis" was the rage of the country, and Summers couldn't help but sing it as he thought about how surprised Laura would be. He sang so loud he didn't hear Sheriff Peterson, the big Swede, come in the front door. Peterson just stared. "Why you talkin' to yourself, Andrew?"

Summers blushed. "Oh, I was just singing, 'Meet Me in St. Louis, Louis.'"

Peterson shook his head. "I heard you singing that foolish "Hoochee Koochee" song. In Sweden we sang happy songs about the joy of work, but here in America you sing about anything *but* work."

Regaining his composure, Summers shrugged. "That's America, and I guess that's why you're here."

"I came to work and I work," Peterson said indignantly.

"Well, I got my own work to do," Summers said, "so unless you got something to say, I'd like to get back to earning my American living."

Peterson cleared his throat. "You call singing work?"

"I'm researching a story," Summers retorted, then sang loudly, "Meet me at the fairrrrrrrrrrrrrrr!" He held the last note as long as he could.

Peterson mumbled something in Swedish and left. "Hey, Sheriff," Summers called out, "what'd you want?" But the sheriff didn't hear him, so Summers shrugged and took out the packet of information he had on the fair.

In addition to the international exposition, the 100th anniversary of the Louisiana Purchase was being celebrated in St. Louis. Americans were heading by the trainload to the cotton capital founded by French traders. With 600,000 people and growing daily, St. Louis's high society wanted to show their city to the world. They'd invited virtually the entire list of Europe's royalty and then some.

The rough-and-tumble, newly rich in America were thrilled by the presence of dukes, counts, and princes, as well as several imposters who were wined and dined like royalty. Many of them were broke, looking to marry the daughters and widows of America's new-money elite.

Andrew Jackson Summers read through the history of the song he was humming:

What's Behind That Song You're Singing?

By Jack Dunning

"Meet Me in St. Louis, Louis," the official song of the fair, was written by Andrew B. Sterling. While sitting in a Broadway cafe, he heard a customer ask the waiter, Louis, for another glass of St. Louis Beer. "Another Louis, Louis." Sterling was struck by the phrase and quickly jotted down a verse and rhythm, and the rest is history. Millions of Americans are singing it wherever they go. I've heard that virtually everyone with a gramaphone has a copy of the song.

Summers looked at the note that Dunning attached:

Andy:

The St. Louis World's Fair is going to be one of the grandest spectacles of modern times! St. Louis has gone all out to show itself off to the world.

Electric trains, fans, dishwashers, washing machines, ice-machine air cooling, world-famous choirs, dancers, chorus girls—it is all here. From the weird to the wacky to the wonderful and whatever, the St. Louis World's Fair promises it all and then some. A ten-ton block of cheese, life-sized chocolate statues of famous people, cannons that can shoot twenty miles.

Just like at the Chicago Exposition, people from all over the world will be there. African runners, Japanese wrestlers, Egyptian dancers doing the Hoochee Koochee, bands playing everything from Mississippi delta blues to New Orleans ragtime, and symphony players and concert singers from around the country. This fair is dedicated to fun, fantasy, and the future.

People are coming on steamboats, excursion trains, automobiles, and on horseback. Tell your readers to sell their cookstoves, sell their wagons, cash in their burial plots, sell anything—but don't miss this show of all shows.

Jack

Summers smiled. *Jack must have taken a course in puffery writing from P. T. Barnum.* But he had to admit it sounded exciting. *Sounds like a good place to send Laura,* he thought. And again, he sang the song he couldn't get out of his mind.

> Meet me in St. Louis, Louis,
> Meet me at the fair,

Don't tell me the lights are shining
Any place but there.
We will dance the Hoochee Koochee,
I will be your tootsie wootsie,
If you will meet me in St. Louis, Louis,
Meet me at the fair.

CHAPTER 5

SKIPPIN' FEVER

Six-year-old Terry Youngun, son of Rev. Thomas Youngun, the widower Methodist minister of Mansfield, Missouri, lay in his bed moaning.

"Where does it hurt, son?" Rev. Youngun asked.

"All over. It feels like I've been runned over by a fire wagon." Terry moaned again loudly for effect. He was putting on the best act he could because he wasn't sick from anything —except sick of school.

Terry had sneaked down early in the morning and removed the rock he'd put in the heating stove, wrapped it up in a cloth, and hid it under his pillow. With the wet cloth he'd hidden in the bowl under the bed, he'd managed to put on a convincing sweating fever.

"I think I should stay home, Pa. Don't want to give anyone my zeeze."

"That's disease," his father corrected him. He looked down and felt his son's head. "It feels a bit warm. Hmmmm, maybe you should stay in bed for the day."

"I think so, Pa," Terry moaned, crossing his fingers and toes under the covers.

His nine-year-old brother, Larry, looked in. His soon-to-be-five-year-old sister, Sherry, peeked below Larry's arm. "Are you goin' to let him stay home, Pa?" Larry asked.

Rev. Youngun shrugged. "His head feels hot. I don't want him spreadin' a fever to the other children."

"But, Pa," Larry protested, "if he stays home, I want to stay home."

"Me too!" said Sherry.

Rev. Youngun patted Terry on the head and stepped toward the door. "Sometimes we all get sick. We can't change the course of nature."

Terry stuck his tongue out at his sister. "Pa!" she screamed, but by the time his father turned, Terry's head was back under the covers.

As the door closed, Larry shook his head. "I think he's alternatin' the course of nature."

"You mean 'altering,' and why would he want to do that? Who wants to be sick?" Rev. Youngun asked.

Larry sighed. "That's the point. He ain't sick! It's a beautiful spring day out and he just wants to play hooky and go fishin'."

Sherry spit on her hands and slapped them together. "I'm goin' to go in there and call him fibber and—"

Rev. Youngun grabbed his feisty daughter by the collar of her school dress. "Quit that spitting on your hands. You're not goin' to bother Terry. I think he's sick. I want you both to leave him alone."

Larry got on his tippy toes and whispered into his father's ear. "Pa, listen. Let's stomp our feet and pretend we're goin' downstairs. Then peek into his room. I know that squirrel's fakin'. I just know it."

Rev. Youngun thought about it for a moment, then whispered, "All right, let's try it once."

Larry shouted out, "Come on, Pa, let's eat breakfast. I can't wait to go to school."

"Me too," Sherry shouted.

"Okay, children, let's leave Terry alone. I don't want anybody bothering him for the rest of the day. I've got to go into town now and won't be back until supper."

Sherry giggled as the three of them stomped loudly, pretending to march down the stairs, then turned and tiptoed back and stood quietly outside Terry's bedroom door.

Terry looked up from the covers and listened to them march downstairs. It worked! He'd fooled Pa and could stay home for the day!

He sat up and looked out the window. It *was* a great spring day. Birds were chirping, there was a slight breeze in the air. It was the perfect day to go fishing and swimming down at the Willow Creek Bridge.

He shook his fist in the air like he'd seen baseball players do and skipped around the room singing, "No school, school's for fools, don't want to learn no spellin' rules."

In his mind he saw everything he wanted to do that day, but he didn't see the crack in the door and the six eyes watching him. It was on the third skip around the room that he heard his father clear his throat. He turned and saw the opened door.

"Terry, what are you doing?"

Larry stood up. "Pa, he's—"

Rev. Youngun clamped his hand on Larry's mouth. "I asked what you're doing?"

Terry put his brain in overdrive to think of a way out. "Ah, Pa, I think the fever's possessed me. Yup, it's makin' me do crazy things."

His father crossed his arms, knowing that his son was up to his tricks again. "It is, huh?"

Terry closed his eyes and moaned. "It's the skippin' fever that's got me, Pa. It comes from too much studyin'. Can't tell when it's goin' to—" Terry spun around and grabbed his forehead. "It's got me again, Pa! I feel another skippin' bout comin' on."

Terry began skipping around the room with his eyes closed. Faster and faster he went, until he crashed into his dresser. Rev. Youngun just shook his head.

"Breakfast will be served in ten minutes. See if you can get over your skippin' fever and be dressed in time."

As the door closed behind him, Terry hit his fist into his palm. "Rats! I blew it! Could have gone fishin' all day, but no, I got to skip around the room." He shook his head and began dressing. It was no use pretending: He had been caught.

Ten minutes later, Terry came into the kitchen and sat at the table as if nothing had happened. "Can I go swimmin' after school, Pa?"

Rev. Youngun shook his head. "I think you need to wait a day to get over the skippin' fever—and to learn that lying is wrong."

"But, Pa—?"

"No buts about it. You come right home from school and clean the yard. Now, who wants to say the blessing?"

Terry dropped his napkin, which was number six on his list of a thousand ways of getting out of saying grace. Larry just looked up at the ceiling, hoping his father wouldn't pick him.

"I do!" little sister squealed.

Rev. Youngun looked at his auburn-haired son. "How about you, Terry? Don't you hear the Spirit calling you?"

Terry stuck his finger in his ear and pulled out some wax. "Sorry, Pa, but my ear's so clogged with wax, I can't hear a thing. What did you say?"

Beezer, the big green parrot that Uncle Cletus had left with them, walked into the room, climbed up on his perch, and squawked, "Say your prayers!"

They all turned and laughed. Rev. Youngun said, "Beezer's right, Terry. Don't you want to say your prayers?"

"Still feel kind of sick, Pa." He stopped when he saw the look on his father's face. "Let Sherry, Pa. She wants to."

"Never mind, how 'bout you Larry?"

"Sherry asked first, Pa."

"Let me, Pa, please let me!" Sherry begged.

As always, Sherry wanted to say it—or perhaps more accurately, sing it. You see, you never knew if Sherry was going to recite a one- or five-minute grace filled with all kinds of wild things, or whether she would sing one to the tune of a song she knew.

"Okay, Sherry, say a short and sweet one," her father said, crossing his fingers in hope.

They all closed their eyes and clasped their hands. Terry and Larry looked at each other, knowing they were in for a long one as Sherry began:

"God, Maker of everything including Tootsie Rolls and Coca Colas, we love you and miss you." She paused for breath. "Lord who made pretty girls like me and who made all the trees and birds and bugs and rocks and horses and clowns and . . . and . . . and dogs and cats and snails and even bad boys like Terry and baseballs and big brothers like Larry and thank you for giving us this day our jelly bread and . . ."

Rev. Youngun opened his eyes as she paused and caught her breath. Everyone hoped she had run out of gas. Terry was mimicking her, and Larry was staring at the food.

Then she began again, but this time Rev. Youngun helped bring her prayer to a close with a forceful, "Amen!" He raised his hands and clapped once. "Eat now or you'll be late for school."

Corn bread, sliced cheese, apples, and hard-boiled eggs was the best breakfast he could make. Rev. Youngun had never been much of a cook, but the kids tolerated it because they were in no rush for their Pa to bring home a new mom.

Dangit the dog pawed at the back door. "I'll let him in,"

Larry said, getting up from the table. The dog flew through the open door and crawled under the breakfast table. Terry immediately slipped Dangit a piece of cheese.

Rev. Youngun shook his head. "I don't like you feeding Dangit at the table."

"Sorry, Pa."

Larry looked at *The Mansfield Monitor,* which was spread out on the counter. The newspaper was opened to the full-page ad for the Mansfield dog show.

"Pa, what's a dog show?"

Rev. Youngun wasn't paying much attention. "That's where people enter their dogs in competition against other dogs."

"What kind of competition?" Larry asked. "Fightin' and pullin'?"

Rev. Youngun laughed. "No, no. They're judged on looks, intelligence, grooming—that sort of thing."

Larry walked over and looked under the table at Dangit, who was eating another piece of Terry's cheese. "Can we enter Dangit, Pa?"

"I don't think they're giving out prizes for the most ornery dog."

"Prizes!" Terry exclaimed. "What kind of prizes?"

Larry walked back over and looked at the paper. "Says here the winner of the dog show that Mrs. Bentley is sponsoring will get fifty dollars and a trip to St. Louis to compete in the World's Fair dog show where . . ." He paused and looked at the paper as if he couldn't believe his eyes. "The prize in St. Louis *is one thousand dollars!*"

"*One thousand dollars!*" Terry shouted. "Man, we'd be on easy street for the rest of our lives." He looked at his father with wide eyes. "We could hire you to do nothin' but pray for us!"

"That's all I seem to do now anyway," Rev. Youngun said with a sigh.

"What'd you say, Pa?" Larry asked.

"Nothing."

"Can we enter Dangit?" Larry asked, looking at the paper. "Says it only costs one dollar to enter."

"That's a lot of money, son."

Terry looked at Dangit. "It'd be an investment. Heck, put in a dollar and get back fifty bucks. I'd do that all day long for the rest of my life."

Rev. Youngun smiled. "There's no guarantee Dangit will win. Just because you think he's beautiful doesn't mean everyone else will."

"Pa!" Larry said, picking up Dangit, who looked like a chipmunk with his cheeks stuffed with food. "How can you say he's not beautiful?"

Rev. Youngun wanted to laugh but held it back. He looked at the mutt the kids loved and shook his head. "Beauty certainly *is* in the eye of the beholder, isn't it?"

Terry nodded. "It sure is and Dangit's beautiful." He looked at Dangit. "Say, what you got in your mouth, boy?" Dangit opened his jaws and a whole, unpeeled hardboiled egg rolled out and cracked on the floor.

"You're pathetic!" Beezer squawked.

Rev. Youngun stood up. "You children clean your plates and get ready for school."

"Fur-get it! School's for fools!" Beezer squawked.

Rev. Youngun thought he knew every one of Beezer's phrases, but he hadn't heard these. Sherry giggled. "Terry's been teachin' Beezer some new talk."

"Just don't let me catch you teachin' him a swear word, or Beezer will be sleeping out in the barn with the cats. Now clear the table and get on to school."

As he left the room, Larry looked at the ad again and then back to Dangit. "Boy, you're goin' to win us some big bucks."

He began moving his fingers like he was counting money. "One thousand dollars. We'll be rich!"

"Too rich to go to school," Terry nodded. "With that much money, I'll just crown myself king of Mansfield and eat nothin' but candy and only drink Cokes."

CHAPTER 6

THE SURPRISE

Laura was running a little late. When she didn't show up at the office on time, Summers called Apple Hill Farm. "Manly, this is Summers. Where's Laura?"

"She ought to be there soon."

"Good. 'Cause I want to surprise her with the St. Louis assignment."

"St. Louis?"

"Yeah. I want her to go to St. Louis, to the World's Fair and the Olympics."

Manly's eyebrows raised up. "By herself? That's a big city for her to be all alone and—"

Summers cut him off. "Oh, bullfeathers! She'll be part of the newspeople covering the story. Why, there'll be a hundred or so top newsmen there."

Manly, who thought that most newspaper men were drunkards and skirt chasers, wasn't very pleased. "I don't think it's a good idea, Summers. Laura's got too much work to do around here."

Summers laughed heartily. "Why, Manly Wilder, I think you're jealous!"

Manly was irritated by his boisterous laugh. "All right, you're right! I don't want her goin' off by herself to the big city."

Summers laughed again. "I can only pay for one ticket. I've booked her at a fine hotel."

Manly suddenly had an idea. "I'll make you a deal, Summers. I'll buy my own ticket and pay the extra costs at the hotel and go along with her."

"You go along? This isn't a pleasure trip."

"Look, Summers, she'll get her writing done."

"I thought you hated big cities."

"I do. But Laura and me, well, she never got the big city honeymoon I promised her almost twenty years ago."

Summers shook his head. "Look, I don't care what you want to call the trip. I want Laura to cover the story, and I have no problem with you goin' if you pay your own way."

"Just don't tell her. I want to surprise her, okay?"

"Whatever you say, Romeo."

"Cut it out. Just tell me when's the trip and what hotel."

"Let me see, where did I write it down? Here it is. She leaves this Saturday and is booked at the Ritz for three nights."

"Thanks, Summers. Thanks for calling."

Manly hung up and didn't hear Summers shouting, "Hey. Hey Manly, I still don't know where—"

Summers put the phone down and looked up at the sound of the tinkling bell over the door. "Hello Laura. How are you?"

"My neck hurts, I had an argument this morning with Manly, and I never had a honeymoon. Now is there anything you want me to write about, or can I go home and start the day over?" she said.

Summers smiled. "Can't help what's happened, but I can make your day. How'd you like to go to St. Louis?"

"St. Louis? What for?"

"I want you to go to the World's Fair."

Laura was in shock. "The World's Fair? Why I hear it costs a fortune. And there isn't a hotel room around for miles that's not booked."

"Be quiet for a change, will you? Come here and read some of this. I want you to go to St. Louis and write about it. All expenses paid," he said proudly.

"Are you feeling all right, Andrew? Why aren't you going?"

"Can't. Got some business with the bank to attend to. But you need a change of scenery and it'll do you good to see what goes on in the big city."

While Laura heard about her assignment to cover the St. Louis World's Fair and the Third Olympics, Manly was on the phone, dialing Stephen Scales, the town telegraph operator. "Stephen, this is Manly. I need you to send a telegram to the Ritz Hotel in St. Louis."

"The Ritz? Who you know that's stayin' there? Why that place costs probably ten bucks a night!"

"Hush, will ya'? I'm stayin' there."

"If you're stayin' there, why do you need me to send a telegram?"

Manly sighed. "Just shush and listen. I'm not there yet but I'm goin'. I want you to telegraph 'em and tell 'em to change the room for Laura Wilder to the honeymoon suite."

"Honeymoon suite!" "Ain't you a little old for that? You got the fever or somethin'? Been eatin' too many hill berries? Dr. George said they do strange things to men 'bout your age."

Manly was so frustrated he wanted to hang up. But there was only one telegraph operator in town, so he had no choice but to endure Scale's ignorant talk. "Stephen, I made Laura a promise that she'd have a honeymoon."

"When?"

"When I married her."

"That must have been about twenty-five years ago. She must have a memory like an elephant."

Manly was getting a headache. "Stephen, you're never too old to keep a promise. Just wire the Ritz that Laura and I will be arrivin' tomorrow afternoon, and I want flowers and champagne waitin' in the room. I'll pay cash when I get there."

"Champagne? What's gotten into you? I thought you were a teetotaler?"

"It's just something that honeymoons are supposed to have. I read it in *Ladies Home Journal* this morning."

"You read *Ladies Home Journal?*" Scales said, laughing.

"Weren't nothin' else to read, sittin' in the privy. Look, will you just send the telegram? I'll stop by later and pay you."

"Manly Wilder, I've never heard you talk like this before. Honeymoon, flowers, champagne—you sure you're feelin' alright?"

"I guess I'm kind of excited thinkin' 'bout it. And yes-sir-re, you're also never too old for a honeymoon."

CHAPTER 7

TELLIN' A WHOPPER!

T erry kicked a can as he walked home from school. *I know Pa said I couldn't go swimming today. He's still mad at me for tellin' him I had skippin' fever. Might as well be puttin' me in prison.* He frowned, shaking his head.

Little James and Frenchie ran by. "Last one in the river's a rotten egg!" Frenchie screamed.

"Ain't you goin' swimmin'?" Little James stopped and asked.

"Naw," Terry said, kicking the can high into the air. "Got some things I gotta do at home."

"Too bad," Little James said. "You're missin' out on all the fun."

Terry watched his friend run off. *Pa will never know. How will he find out if I sneak a quick swim in?* He looked at his brother Larry, walking ahead of him. *Larry will rat on me. That's how he'll find out. Sometimes he's worse than Sherry. Musta gotten bit by the honest bug when he was a baby or somethin'.*

There was only one thing to do. Terry decided to talk his brother into going swimming. *He ain't gonna rat on himself.*

That'd be suicide. So I'll just talk him into what he wants to be talked into. "Hey, Larry, I got somethin' I wanna ask you," he shouted, racing ahead.

"Come on, Larry. Pa'll never know," Terry pleaded, as they reached the edge of their property. With the house looming, Terry knew he had only a minute or two to talk Larry into the swimming fib.

"He told us not to," Larry said, wanting to go but not wanting to disobey their father.

"What he don't know won't hurt him, and if he don't ask later you won't have to lie. Okay?"

Larry looked at his brother and the sunny, warm day outside. He thought how good the creek would feel. "Okay, but just for a little while, and we do our chores first and leave the creek when I say so."

"You got it!" Terry agreed, and ran with his brother to clean up the barn.

What the boys didn't know was that their father had made a point of taking their swimsuits so they wouldn't be tempted to disobey. He was proud that after doing their chores, they didn't fight it, and went off to play in the woods. But that was just pretend. Once out of his sight, the brothers headed right to Willow Creek Bridge and jumped in naked.

"Man, this feels great!" Terry shouted, swimming around like an otter.

Larry had to agree, but he was still worried that their father would find out. They hadn't brought Sherry along because she'd tell on them for sure. But if his father didn't ask, then they wouldn't have to fib. And not fibbing made disobeying Pa's order not to go swimming seem only half as bad.

They had a glorious time, swimming and diving. Terry found a rock that looked like an arrowhead, and stuck it in his pants' pocket on the creek bank. Terry had a way of saving things and finding uses for them later.

Larry was standing on the branch of the overhanging tree they liked to jump from when his worst nightmare came true. "Yo-hoo," shouted Missouri Poole from the edge of the creek, "I see you."

"Who said that?" Larry shouted, looking around and trying to cover himself as best he could.

"Hey, Sugar, it's me, your girlfriend. Missouri."

Larry took a step to look around the tree, but with his hands busy trying to cover up, he slipped and fell off the branch, landing in the water with a big splash. When he came to the surface, he kept his eyes just above the water like an alligator.

Terry swam over. "What's she doin' here?"

"How should I know."

Terry shrugged in the water. "Did she see you necked?"

"I don't think so," Larry said, looking around for Missouri.

Terry shook his head. "If she saw me naked as a jaybird, I'd be too embarrassed to ever go back to school again. Ain't no girl gonna ever see me without my clothes on."

Larry looked at Terry. "Sherry's seen you."

Terry took a mouthful of water and spit it in his brother's face. "She don't count."

"Hey, Larry," Missouri shouted from somewhere in the bushes. "I saw you naked."

Larry blushed and sank under the water. When he came up, Terry sighed. "Oh man! Now you can't *ever* go back to school."

"I don't believe her. She's lyin'."

Missouri called out again. "I like the mole on your rump," she said with a laugh.

"I believe her," Terry said. "You *do* have a mole back there."

"What am I gonna do?"

Terry took a deep breath and blew it out, fluttering his lips.

"You can either quit school or die. Those are the only choices you got."

"You're crazy!" Larry said, looking around for Missouri.

"Course if it were me, why I'd just quit school. Ain't worth dyin' over. Yup, only thing you can do is . . . quit school."

"Can't quit school!" Larry said. "I ain't even reached the fifth grade yet!"

"You gotta. Everyone's gonna know that she saw you necked. Shoot, she knows about the mole on your behind, so no tellin' what else she saw." Terry paused and put on a deadly serious face. "'Course she wants to marry you and all, so maybe you ought to just get married and move into her house. That way I can have the bedroom all to myself."

Larry pushed Terry's head down under the water. When Terry came up, Larry said, "No one will believe her anyway. I'll just say there ain't no truth to it. That she was never near our swimmin' hole."

"You'd be the one lyin', Mister Goody-Two-Shoes."

Larry thought about it. Lying was bad, but having a girl see you naked was worse. "Sometimes you got to lie."

"I've been tellin' you that for a long time," Terry nodded.

"You like to fib 'bout everythin'," Larry said. "It's your fault that this all happened, anyway!" He frowned at what his brother had gotten him into.

Terry spit water into his brother's face again. "At least you know where I stand on things."

Larry felt better. "No one's gonna believe Missouri Poole. Yup, no one will believe her. Let's go."

Larry started forward and then he saw her. Missouri was standing on the edge of the creek, waving his underbritches around.

"I'm goin' to take these home and keep 'em," and she laughed, spinning around in her long, homemade, butternut dress.

"Don't," he said, his mouth dropping.

"Or maybe I'm gonna take them to school. Let's see," she said, looking at the underpants. "Yup, says *Larry* right here. Written proof that I'm tellin' the truth, right on the flap."

"Your goose is cooked," Terry whispered, swimming away from his brother.

"Where you goin'?" Larry whispered.

"You think I want to hang 'round with a guy who lets a girl steal his undies?"

Larry was in a fix. "Missouri, please don't take 'em!"

"Why not?" she asked, tossing his underbritches up in the air.

" 'Cause I'm askin' you not to."

Missouri looked at him. "I'm still mad that you didn't give me my Valentine's kiss."

From behind him he heard a wolf whistle. Terry was making faces at him. Larry thought fast. "If you take my underbritches, then I'll have to quit school and move away. You'd never, ever see me again."

Missouri called his bluff. "I'll have your undies to remember you by."

Larry was stumped. "Please, Missouri. Come on."

"I'll give 'em back to ya' if you kiss me."

Larry was boxed in. Kissing her was better than her having his underbritches. "Okay."

Missouri brightened. "Well come on out here and kiss me."

"Missouri!" Larry shouted, trying his best to sound embarrassed. *"I got to get dressed first."*

That was reasonable to Missouri. "All right, I'll leave your clothes on the rock where I found 'em. I'll be waitin' for my kiss behind the tree."

Larry was relieved. "Keep your eyes closed."

He winked at Terry and the two of them swam underwater to the edge of the creek. They got dressed in lightning-fast

time. Terry didn't even realize that his shirt was inside out. All he wanted to do was get far away from this nosey girl.

"You gonna kiss her?" Terry whispered.

"Naw," Larry whispered back. "I just said that to get my undies back."

"But that's a *fib*," Terry said, mocking his older brother.

"Better to fib than to have her showin' my undies off to everyone."

"Least there weren't nothin' in the back of 'em."

"Oh, man," Larry said. "I *would* have to quit school then."

Missouri called out, "Ready?"

Terry pushed Larry forward. "Go on. Kiss her and get it over with. Can't be worse than kissing . . ." He paused to watch Dangit running up the creek bank. "Than kissing Dangit."

Dangit jumped into Larry's arms, which gave him an idea. "Hey Missouri, you promise to keep your eyes closed?" Larry asked.

"I promise," she called back.

"Here I come," Larry said. He whispered into Dangit's ear, "Be good. Her lips ain't worse'n eatin' a dead fish."

Larry walked quietly around the tree with Dangit in his arms, then stopped dead in his tracks. It was a bad dream, staring him in the face. Missouri was waiting for him with her eyes closed and lips puckered. "Just one kiss," Larry said, approaching as carefully as he could in case she jumped for him.

"One kiss is enough for now," she said, giggling.

"Here goes," Larry said. He held Dangit up to her face and put his dog lips on Missouri's.

"Keep your eyes closed," he whispered.

"They're closed. Hurry, I've been dreamin' of this," she said with a smile.

Missouri reached forward, thinking she was really going to

kiss Larry, but all she grabbed was Dangit, who began licking all over her face.

"Larry Youngun! Dangit, I'm gonna get you!" she shouted, dropping Dangit like a hot potato and coming toward Larry.

Dangit, who didn't like to be dropped and really didn't like her misusing his name, grabbed the end of Missouri's long dress and spun her around.

"Come on," Terry shouted, pulling his brother along, "let's get outta here!"

While Dangit pulled Missouri in circles, the Younguns doubled back through the woods and ran toward their house. Terry looked around for their father, then whispered, "Remember, we've been playin' Davy Crockett and Daniel Boone."

"I don't like it," Larry whispered back.

"You ain't got no choice," Terry said. "Just be glad you got your undies on. You could be dead or married by now."

"Is that you, boys?"

"Ah-oh, Pa's comin'," Larry whispered, his eyes as wide as silver dollars.

Terry looked at their clothes. Then felt his hair. *Think, think of something to say,* he told himself.

Their father came out and looked them up and down. He noticed their damp hair. "Terry, have you been swimming?"

Terry hadn't learned yet that it's worse to lie than to be switched. He had always operated under what he called Terry Youngun's First Commandment—*Thou Shalt Not Get Caught.*

"No, Pa, I ain't. Me and Larry been playin' Crockett and Boone. We beat the Indians this time, we sure did."

Larry looked down and all around, everywhere except into his father's eyes. Terry's tall tales always embarrassed him. Rev. Youngun could look into Larry's eyes and know when he had a guilty conscience. It was one of the ways he kept up with Terry's antics. "Are you sure that's what you boys were doing?"

Terry began his historical fib. "Yes sir, Pa, we were doin' what we read 'bout in school." He winked at his father. "You'd have been proud of us, seein' how much we'd learned in school. I was ol' Davy Crocket and Larry was Danny Boone. We were recreatin' our history lessons, yes we were."

"Such devotion to your studies," Rev. Youngun said, nodding as if impressed. "Hardly seems like you've got time to play and enjoy yourselves."

Terry nodded. "That is somethin' I've been meanin' to talk with you 'bout. Kids need time just to play, but Larry and me, all we seem to do is work work work, study study study, and sleep sleep sleep."

"I see," Rev. Youngun said sympathetically. "My, my, my. You boys are really sweating. I didn't think it was so hot out there."

"Not too hot, Pa," Terry said, not catching the hidden meaning like Larry did. Larry just closed his eyes, knowing they'd been caught.

Rev. Youngun touched their wet heads. "But your hair's wet?"

Larry lowered his head, but Terry kept going. "Oh that," he laughed, like it was no big deal. "We were runnin' so hard we just worked up a sweat."

Rev. Youngun looked down at their wet clothes and the water drops on the floor around them. "You sure did. Why, you boys seem to be wet all over."

"That's 'cause we were recreatin' history so hard. We fought the Indians like Crockett and Boone did."

"You did? And that's how you worked up such a sweat?"

Terry nodded. "Why, Larry said we were doin' so good that we might just show the teacher how you learn more study-playin' than sittin' in class."

Larry took a deep breath and looked away. They were already in deep trouble, and Terry was digging a moat filled with fib-eatin' crocodiles all around them. He couldn't believe how Terry, once he got started, could just go on and on, never seeing the edge of the cliff up ahead.

"And look, Pa," Terry said, "I even found an arrowhead." He grinned, pulling from his pocket the pointed rock he'd found. "I think it's the real thing. Probably worth enough money for you to take us down to Bedal's General Store to buy some ice cream."

He held it up, admiring it like it was the world's greatest treasure, then handed it to his father. "You keep it, Pa. Maybe it'll bring enough money to help some poor people in the county."

Rev. Youngun clicked his tongue and shook his head, like he wished he could keep it but couldn't. "I think you ought to keep it to remember this day by."

Terry just couldn't seem to stop, and after enough fibs, yarns, and tall tales to weigh down a ten-pound fanny paddle, Rev. Youngun hit him with the big one. "I'm going to ask you just one more time, Terry, have you been swimming?"

"No, Pa, I said I hadn't. I'm wet from sweatin', that's all."

"Well, how did your shirt get wrong side out?"

Terry looked down at his shirt. *I put it on inside out. Oh man, what am I going to do now?* A quick glance toward big brother, angel Larry, who would rather tell the truth and take his punishment, told Terry where he stood.

The only thing to do was to follow what he called Terry Youngun's Second Commandment—*Get as close to the truth as you can.*

"Pa, I was climbing through a hole in the fence backwards and that's how my shirt got inside out."

This child is amazing, Rev. Youngun thought. "Come with me," he said, taking Terry by the hand.

"What, Pa? Where you takin' me?" Terry said, looking at Larry who was shaking his head.

"You know," Rev. Youngun said, dragging Terry by the hand.

Behind the barn, Rev. Youngun picked up a switchin' stick and shook his head. "This is going to hurt me as much as it's goin' to hurt you."

"Now, you're fibbin', Pa."

Rev. Youngun nodded. "You're probably right."

"You shouldn't switch children," Terry said, pleading with his father.

"And you shouldn't lie."

Rev. Youngun stood there and stared. *My father switched me, but the only thing I learned was fear. My mother talked to me about the difference between right and wrong, then made me write one hundred times what I'd done wrong.*

He decided to take his mother's route and took Terry for a walk-and-talk about why lying is bad. Hoping for the best, he sent Terry to his room. "Now, I want you to write one hundred times that you won't lie."

"One hundred times! Gosh, Pa, that's a lot."

"Would you rather be switched?"

"I'll take my chance with the pencil," Terry said with a shrug, and he skipped up the stairs.

CHAPTER 8

LEAVING HOME

aura sat in a rocker on the front porch, reading the information on the St. Louis assignment. The thought of going to cover the World's Fair was exciting. *It does make me a bit nervous, though, going to a big city by myself. But I'm sure everything will be all right.*

Manly was acting strange. She had expected him to be dead set against the trip, but instead, he encouraged her to go. "I think it's wonderful," he told her. "Go on, have a great time! You deserve it."

That wasn't like Manly. *Does he want me to go away?* she thought to herself. *Is something wrong?*

Manly had just walked off to the back pasture to bring in the cows, whistling like her going off to a big city by herself was something she did every day. No matter how hard she tried to concentrate on the material Summers had given her, Laura couldn't think straight.

Manly is definitely up to something, she decided.

Maurice Springer, their black farm neighbor and sometimes laborer, rode up on his wagon to deliver the feed Manly had purchased from him. "Mornin', Laura," he said, stepping off.

"Well, good morning to you Maurice."

"Is there somethin' botherin' you?" Maurice asked with a concerned look on his face.

Laura shrugged. "I've got to go to St. Louis by myself and it doesn't seem to bother Manly at all."

Maurice closed his eyes to think, then opened them smiling. "I think he just loves you so much that he don't want you to know how much he's worried 'bout you goin'."

That sounds like Manly, she thought. "I hope you're right, Maurice."

Maurice smiled. "Well, you be careful and take care of yourself in St. Louis, you hear?" He got back up on the wagon and rode back to the barn to drop off the feed. He waved as he came back around and rode away.

Laura worried all night over Manly's lackadaisical attitude about her leaving. "You aren't bothered about anything?" she asked over breakfast.

"Only thing I'm bothered about is you missing the train," he said, looking at his watch.

Rose, who was in on the secret, smiled behind her hand. "Really, Mother, you write about women being more assertive and now you're making such a big to-do about this trip."

"Well, it's just that . . ."

Manly got up from his chair and stood behind her. "Don't you worry, Laura. Rose and I can take care of ourselves. We'll do just fine without you."

Rose had to walk out of the room to keep from laughing. Laura sat perplexed, watching Manly take his dishes to the sink and actually begin cleaning them. It was as if he'd been hit over the head with a hammer and had changed his personality completely.

"Yes sir, this is a new world for me," he said, scrubbing the food off his plate. "Think I'll try makin' my own clothes while you're gone."

Laura turned away, and Manly had to hide his face to keep from laughing out loud. She got up quietly and said, "I guess you can do it all without me."

Laura walked to the bedroom and strapped up her suitcase. She was so deep in thought that she didn't notice that Manly's drawers were minus his best shirt, and his Sunday suit wasn't hanging in the closet.

Rose came up behind her father and whispered, "Where'd you put your suitcase?"

"I hid it under the spare tire. She'll never think to look in there."

Rose giggled. "How are you going to get on the train without her seeing you."

Manly smiled. "I worked it out with Stephen down at the train station. He's gonna put me up front with the engineer. That way I can get off the train first in St. Louis and hightail it to the hotel and be waitin' for your ma."

Rose hugged him. "I think you're wonderful, Father."

But for Laura the ride to the station was like a funeral procession. She was as solemn as a grieving relative. *Why are they talking up a storm as if they were going to the county fair?*

Laura huffed. "You two act like you're glad to be getting rid of me. Maybe I should tell Summers to send someone else."

Manly shook his head. "Now lookey here, Miss Right-To-Vote. This is the kind of thing you've been advocatin' for, for years. Women goin' off on their own to make their way in the world."

"He's right, Mother. You're going away on business, setting an example for millions of women and—"

Laura cut her off. "I don't feel like an example right now. As a matter of fact, I'm feeling like you two don't need me around."

Manly hugged her. "Just go off and do your newspaperin' job. Course we'll miss you, but you always said that husbands have to learn to take care of house things."

"But . . ." she stammered.

"No buts about it. You go on and write up a storm. I'll stay behind on Apple Hill and do the cookin' and cleanin'."

"He'll be a regular homebody, Mother," Rose laughed.

"Hush, Rose!" Manly snapped. "I don't want nobody to hear you talkin' like that. I'd never hear the end of it down at the feed store."

Laura nuzzled her head against his neck. "I wish you were coming, Manly. St. Louis is such a big city. It could be that honeymoon we never had and . . ." She sat up suddenly. "Why don't you come, Manly? We could finally have our big-city honeymoon."

Manly shook his head sadly. "Sorry, sugar, wish I could. But I promised Maurice that I'd help him plow the fields down along the creek bottom."

Laura didn't say another word until they got to the station. She didn't want to let on how sad she really was. "Well, good-bye, Manly Wilder."

Manly wanted to laugh but kept himself composed. "Come on, Laura. Give me a kiss good-bye. You'll only be gone a few days."

"All right," she said sadly, and pecked him on the cheek.

"We'll miss you, Mother. We really will," Rose said.

"Sure we will," Manly smiled. "But we just want what's best for you."

Laura took the hand of the conductor and stepped up onto the train. "I'll see you both in a few days. Take care of yourselves," she said, feeling her eyes well up. She turned and walked into the train, not wanting Manly to see the tears streaming down her face.

Rose frowned. "I think she's really upset. Why don't you go tell her what you've got planned."

"And spoil the surprise?" Manly exclaimed. "I gotta hurry and get up there with the engineer." Manly ran back to their car and got his suitcase, then sneaked around the station, out of sight of Laura's seat on the train. He climbed up front with the engineer and smiled. "Let's go!" he laughed.

As the train pulled away, Laura sat wiping the tears away, watching Mansfield fall behind. The conductor came through the door. "Magazines? Who wants to read a magazine?"

Laura lifted up her hand and the conductor stopped. She wanted something to take her mind off Manly, marriage, and the honeymoon she never had.

"What do you want, lady?"

"Do you have *Ladies Home Journal*?"

The conductor leafed through the stack of magazines he was carrying and found one. "That'll be ten cents."

Laura got a dime from her purse and bought the magazine. As the conductor went on his way, she opened the magazine to a romance story and began reading.

What a wedding it would be, Julie thought. And what a mansion! Claude had done everything he'd promised and then some.

Claude walked behind her and stroked her long, silky hair. "My dear, why don't we go around the world twice on our honeymoon? We could spend a month in Paris, tour the Rhine, take the train across Russia to the Forbidden City, and eat thousand-year-old bird's nest soup!

"Oh, Claude, you are such a dear! I'm so lucky to have such a warm, considerate man. How can I ever repay you for making all my dreams come true?"

"Just love me," Claude said, kissing behind her ear.
"I do, Claude . . . I do."

Other people honeymooning was not something she wanted to think about, so she flipped through to another story called, "Our House."

"Karen, forgive me. I don't want you to leave our house." Karen looked at her husband of thirty years and shook her head, letting her still-beautiful curls unfurl around her head.
"We were happy once, weren't we, Charles?"
"Oh yes, Karen, and we can still be. Let me stop working, right this instant. I'll sell the farm and take you on a trip. Just you and I together. To some fabulous city you've always wanted to visit."
"Oh, Charles, would you do that for me?"
"I would do anything for you, anything! Let's make it the honeymoon we never had! Just you and I together, in love, and loving like we used to."

Laura closed up the magazine and rested her head against the window. *Oh, Manly,* she thought, *why couldn't you have been like Charles and come to St. Louis with me?*

Up in the locomotive, the engineer spit some chew juice into the pot by his chair. "You sure are goin' out of your way to surprise your wife."

"I got to keep a promise I made to her."

The engineer shook his head. "I promised my old lady that I'd give her the moon. There are some promises you can't deliver on."

Manly shrugged. "And there are some you can. I promised my wife a big-city honeymoon and she's gonna have it. Just she and I together, alone like we used to be."

The engineer shook his head. "Them things are okay in the beginning, when you don't know each other well enough. But I've been married thirty years this June, and I wouldn't know what to say to my old lady if we were alone more than a day."

Manly stood by the door, looking out at the Missouri countryside. "We just got some catching up to do, that's all."

CHAPTER 9

BIG CITY LIFE

As the train neared St. Louis, Laura took a quick glance at the newspaper left on the seat beside her. It seemed that all the people on the train were decked out in their finest, going to enjoy the wonders of the World's Fair.

Laura turned her thoughts to the Third Olympics that were being staged along with the Fair, and jotted down the final corrections on a short article she had been working on. Though she was upset that women had been excluded from this year's Olympics, the thought of men competing equally helped restore some of her faith in humanity. *At the next Olympics, they'll let us enter, and soon we'll have the right to vote in this country.*

THE REVIVAL OF THE OLYMPICS
By Laura Ingalls Wilder

The world was without the Olympic Games for more than fifteen centuries. Sports enthusiasts owe their thanks to a spunky Frenchman named Baron Pierre de Coubertin, who almost single-handedly revived the Olympic festivals.

Born to a family of wealth in 1863, and standing only five feet three inches, the Baron would seem an unlikely candidate for bringing back the athletic events of legends. As a student of public education, he traveled widely in Europe and the United States and became fascinated with the way education and sports are intertwined around the world.

Everywhere, that is, except in his native France.

It was during this time that archaeologists were digging up the ruins of the ancient Greek Olympia. Coubertin, being the curious sort, went to Greece to see the ruins.

He later told a French audience, "As I walked the same ground where Coroebus had raced and Milo had wrestled, I became enthralled by what sports has meant to the world. I believed the revival of celebrating the perfection of amateur sports was necessary to stop the commercialism in sports that was creeping worldwide."

Coubertin became a man with a mission, a man obsessed with bringing back the ancient games. And in 1896, the games were revived in Athens, Greece, where it all began.

Everyone visiting the St. Louis games owes Coubertin a debt of gratitude.

The conductor came barreling through the train car. "St. Louis, next stop. St. Louis, next stop."

The passengers around Laura began assembling their bags and cases. Laura packed away her writing tablet and smoothed out her dress. As the train pulled into the station, she was struck by the banners and signs everywhere. It looked like a combination political rally and Fourth of July festival gone mad.

While Laura waited to get off, Manly jumped down from the engine, his bag in hand, and raced ahead to get a taxi. He looked at the people, people everywhere, and for a moment he was confused.

A dozen white wings—the proud street cleaners of the town —were working along the side of the station. A newsgirl with a flowered hat and long plaid dress was hawking papers to the new arrivals.

"Read all about the Olympics," she screamed out. "Midgets and a Pygmy competing against a giant Indian!"

Manly started to ask the newsgirl a question, but she barreled past him with a newspaper held high. He turned and saw a group of station patrolmen keeping watchful eye on the crowd for pickpockets and gypsies. But their hard, flinty glares made Manly uncomfortable, so he decided against asking them for help.

There's more going on in this small part of St. Louis than in all of Mansfield, Manly thought. He walked without direction, then focused on a newspaper stand with banner headlines in a dozen languages. Manly felt even more confused and out-of-place.

Manly saw what he thought was a friendly sort, waiting by the newspaper stand. "Say, mister," he called out, "can you tell me where I can get a cab to the Ritz?"

The man was a typical ne'er-do-well that flourished in big cities and saw Manly as an easy person to con. "Sure, Mac. My uncle runs the cleanest cab in da city."

Manly smiled. "Where's your uncle's cab?"

"Just give me a buck and I'll have him waitin' out front for ya'."

Manly blinked. "A buck. For gettin' him to wait?"

"Oh no," the man protested as part of his act. "The buck's for the ride to the Ritz, a Coke along the way, and a tip to my uncle and the bell hop who'll carry your bag."

"I'm ready to go," Manly said, taking out a dollar. "Where is he?"

"He'll be right out front in ten minutes waiting for you," the man said, and he took the dollar and walked off.

Manly walked slowly through the crowd, lost in the colors and shouting-match conversations going on all around him. He looked outside for Uncle's cab but felt thirsty, so he turned and asked a pastry vendor where he could get some water.

"In there," he said, pointing back inside the large waiting room of the station. "The public cup's in there."

Laura had written articles about how public drinking cups spread disease, but he was thirsty, so he walked over. There were ten people ahead of him. He watched the man who was using the cup cough like his whole body was coming apart.

Manly paled and left the line without getting a drink. He needed air, and he was still thirsty. He walked over to the ice stand and bought a cold Coke from an aging lady.

"Thanks," Manly said, taking a long swig.

She cackled. "You know that when I first started selling Cokes the stuff was green-colored?"

Manly stopped drinking and looked at the bottle. Satisfied that his was brown, he drank the rest of it down. "That a fact," he said, wiping his lips and handing her the bottle.

"That's a fact," she said. "Put a mouse in it and it would disappear, bones and all, after a few days."

"That a fact," Manly said, looking at his watch and wondering where his cab was.

"It's true. Always wondered what the stuff did to your stomach linin'."

"Hope I don't get a stomachache thinkin' about that mouse," Manly said, and he picked up his bags and headed toward the front of the station. Nine minutes were up according to his pocket watch. *Uncle's cab should be out here,* Manly thought.

After twenty minutes, with no sight of the man, Manly decided he'd probably been had. *Hope Laura never finds out.*

He felt the leg of his pants being pulled and looked down to see a monkey with his hand out. Behind him he heard the strains of an off-key organ grinder, turning his money box that rested on a single peg leg. Manly tried to shoo the monkey away but the organ grinder was saying something to him in a foreign language.

"He's speakin' Italian," a woman said, laughing at the pair. People were watching and snickering at Manly's situation. Finally, he reached in his pocket, pulled out a penny, and put it into the monkey's outstretched hand. The monkey looked at it, then threw it back at Manly! The crowd was howling now.

"Get your durn monkey away from me!" Manly shouted at the organ grinder. The organ grinder shook his fist and screamed back in Italian, which Manly couldn't understand.

From behind him came a booming Irish voice. "I told you to stay away from here!" Manly turned and saw a big, burley policeman barreling through the crowd. The monkey screeched, climbed up, and hid inside the music box.

"Get outta here," the policeman shouted, pushing the organ grinder along. The policeman came back, swinging his baton, and leaned against a lamp pole. His eyes crisscrossed the crowd like a cat looking for sneaking rats.

Manly hesitated, then walked over. "Thanks for helpin'."

Without looking at Manly, the policeman said. "Never give those vendors anything, not even a penny. They'll rob you blind if you turn your back on 'em."

"I'll remember that."

The policeman mumbled more to himself than to Manly. "Law of Ninety-One barred lunatics, polygamists, criminals, and indigents from this country but it doesn't do any good."

"What's that?" Manly asked, trying to be polite.

"We're lettin' in the trash and keepin' out the types that came before who built this country."

Manly, feeling like a stranger in the strangest of lands, decided that agreeing in this situation was better than arguing. "Guess you're right."

The policeman tossed his baton up in the air and caught it halfway down. He continued swinging his club, as if he had nothing else to say. Manly tapped his shoulder. "Say, Officer, I gave a man a buck to find his uncle's cab and he ain't showed up. Anything I can do about it?"

The policeman kept swinging his baton. He twitched his handlebar moustache and shook his head. "You seem to like to give money away, don'tcha?" He looked Manly up and down. "You don't look like a Rockefeller."

"I was lost and the man seemed honest," Manly said sheepishly.

The policeman snorted. "Count it as a cheap lesson learned."

"But a buck is a buck," Manly protested.

"Then go back to the farm, or watch your money and stay away from the bad side of town."

Manly scratched his head. "Where's that?" he asked, looking around. *The whole place looks bad to me so far,* he thought.

The policeman laughed. "You are a country boy, aren't you?"

"I've been to a city before."

"St. Louis is no country farm town. Look over there," he said, pointing across the street. "Just a stone's throw away begins the lowlife side of town."

Manly peered across the street. "What's over there?"

The policeman laughed. "Why, a country rube like you'd be ate by the likes of them! There's alleys filled with roving bloodsuckers and shoulder hitters.

"Bloodsuckers and shoulder hitters?" Manly said, wide-eyed. "I don't know what you're talking about."

The policeman rolled his eyes and patiently explained to Manly that bloodsuckers were muggers and shoulder hitters were smash-and-grab alley hoods.

Manly shook his head. "You need a dictionary to understand it all."

The policeman laughed heartily and slapped Manly across the back. "No, you need a dictionary to hit the bloodsuckers up side the head when they come across your tracks." He looked at Manly and smiled. "Let me get you a cab. What hotel you going to?"

"The Ritz."

"Fancy country man, now aren't you," the policeman smiled.

"Just goin' on my honeymoon," Manly smiled, proudly.

The policeman looked around. "Where's the lucky lady?"

Manly shrugged. "She's somewhere back there on the train. I rode in the locomotive and she sat in the back."

"Are you sure you're ready for a honeymoon?" the policeman asked.

"It's a surprise. She doesn't know anything about it." The policeman just looked at Manly as if he were crazy. "Here's her picture," Manly said, opening up his wallet. "Ain't she pretty?"

"She sure is," the policeman said, stepping forward to flag down an approaching cab. "And you say you're on your honeymoon?"

"We've been waitin' for twenty years. I think I'm about ready for it," Manly smiled.

"That's a long time to wait. Good luck, my patient friend," he said helping Manly into the cab. "You've earned whatever's comin'."

"Thanks," Manly smiled. "What do I owe you?"

"Nothin', just doin' my job." He thought about it for a moment, then whispered into Manly's ear, "But a buck for the policemen's widows and orphans fund would be greatly appreciated."

Manly handed him a dollar and the policeman thanked him,

and began walking away. As Manly's cab pulled down the block, Laura came out front with a porter following behind. She looked around for a cab and then saw the same policeman Manly had been talking to.

"Excuse me officer, but I need a cab to the Ritz. Could you help me."

The policeman recognized Laura from the picture and smiled. "Finally goin' on your honeymoon, are ya'?"

Laura was flabbergasted. "Honeymoon?"

Remembering that Manly had said it was a surprise, the officer hesitated. "Oh, I was just talkin' nonsense." He looked at Laura's upscale outfit and nodded. "A woman like you probably had a big wedding and honeymoon when you got married."

Laura accepted his hand as she stepped into the cab he flagged down. "Never got my honeymoon and probably never will."

The policeman, now sure he had the right woman, said, "You just got to be patient. Give it some time."

"I have," Laura said, getting into the cab. "I think twenty years is long enough."

CHAPTER 10

LAURA'S HONEYMOON

anly's driver took the fast way to the Ritz and after paying and tipping the driver and doorman, Manly stood in front of a spit-and-polish desk clerk with a pencil-thin moustache.

"Can I help you?"

Manly nodded. "You sure can. My name's Manly Wilder and you've got the honeymoon suite waitin' for me."

The desk clerk looked around. "Where's your bride?" he said with a smile.

Manly shrugged. "She's back at the train station, why?"

The desk clerk tried to sound nonchalant. "Oh, it's just that usually, when honeymooners check into the Ritz, why, they're together."

Manly grinned. "Shucks. Laura and I've been livin' together for twenty years. I think a little time apart will do us good before the honeymoon."

The desk clerk looked at Manly, wondering, *Is this the way they honeymoon in the Ozarks?* "Whatever you say, sir."

"She don't know this is her honeymoon," Manly chuckled.

The desk clerk was now convinced he was dealing with a

country boy, through and through. "Just a little spur of the moment thing, sir?" the desk clerk asked, getting the check-in forms in order.

Manly swelled up with pride. "Naw, she's been plannin' it for twenty years."

"Very good, sir," the desk clerk said, handing Manly his change. "Bellhop, take Mr. Wilder to the . . . honeymoon suite."

Manly leaned over the counter. "Remember, she don't know a thing about bein' on her honeymoon, so don't let the cat out of the bag, okay?"

"You can depend on me. Have fun."

Manly smiled. "This will be more fun than a barrel of monkeys. Here's a buck for helpin' me," Manly said, handing him a dollar.

"Thank you, sir," the desk clerk said.

More fun than a barrel of monkeys? the desk clerk thought. *I hope he didn't bring his barn animals along.*

Manly shouted back, "Don't forget, keep it a secret from her."

As Manly walked away, the desk clerk sighed. *I've dealt with dukes, princes, and queens, but that guy tops them all.*

The bellhop winked as they got in the elevator. "This is your honeymoon, huh?"

"Yup." Manly smiled, nodding to the elderly elevator operator.

"What floor?" the old man asked.

"Honeymoon suite," the bellhop said, grinning.

"Where's the lucky lady," the old man asked.

Manly shrugged. "Don't know. On her way here somewhere."

The old man looked perplexed as the elevator pulled slowly toward the top floor. "You get married around here?"

"Naw," Manly sighed, "we got married 'bout twenty years

ago in the Dakota territory. Came by wagon to get to Missouri, we did."

"Didn't know it took that long to get here," the old man mumbled. "You should have taken the train."

"What?" Manly asked as the old man stopped the elevator at the top floor.

"Nothin', nothin'," he mumbled. "You have fun now."

"Thank you," Manly said, handing him a dollar.

"Thank you, sir!" the old man grinned. "This will buy me dinner for a week!"

"I just feel like livin' it up," Manly smiled. "I ain't rich but I can sure try to feel like it for a little while."

The bellhop whispered to the old man as Manly got off. "Can you imagine ridin' in a wagon twenty years to get to your honeymoon hotel?" The old man chuckled and shooed the bellhop along.

The bellhop opened the door. Manly gave him a dollar tip, and the bellhop turned to go. Manly, thinking he was all alone, said out loud, "Anyone else 'round here want a tip?"

"Sir?" asked the bellhop.

Manly wheeled around. "I thought you'd gone back to put your hand out to someone else."

"Sir, I just wanted to see if you needed something else, sir."

"I ain't no English knight, you know."

"Sir?" he said, not understanding.

"Oh, nothing. Say where are the flowers I ordered, and the bottle of fancy French champagne?"

"It will be coming right up, sir."

"Quit sirrin' me, will ya?"

"Yes, sir! Er, I mean, all right."

"That's better." Manly looked into the bathroom and blinked at the shiny gold fixtures. Indoor plumbing had just come to Mansfield but he'd never, ever seen or heard about having gold faucet handles. "This place looks like a bank vault."

"It's all fourteen caret gold plated, sir . . . er, mister."

Manly looked at the bathtub for two and grinned. "Kind of big, ain't it?"

"It's the latest tub for two from Europe. It's a French design," the bellhop said proudly.

"French? How can you tell?" Manly asked, running his hand along the edge.

The bellhop swelled up, happy to share this bit of knowledge. "A French tub slopes in the front. If a tub slopes at *both* ends, why it's a Roman tub."

Manly made a face. "Is there a difference in the water that goes in?"

"No, it's the same."

Manly cut him off. "Well then, a bath's a bath. Only difference between this tub-boat and sittin' in a prairie wash tub is the price of this room."

The bellhop nodded. "I guess you're right . . . uh, mister."

Laura's cabbie had taken her the long way, so he could show off the glittering homes of St. Louis's wealthy. "Yup, lady, this city has everythin' to offer. Why, I've even heard some folks say it should be the capitol of this country."

Laura smiled at his provincial pride, but she had to admit St. Louis had come a long way since its days as a small fur-trading settlement. Strategically located on the west bank of the Mississippi River, near the confluence with the Missouri River, St. Louis had played an important part in America's westward migration.

"Yes, lady, in the early days, this town was mostly French. Then after the Louisiana Purchase Treaty, Americans of all kinds came here."

The cabbie pointed out the French influence on the quaint,

native architecture, then took her down Walsh's Row, a fashionable area. Laura was amazed at the size of the homes. The Shaw house on Tower Grove Boulevard, the Campbell House on Locust Place, and the Taj Majhal of Saint Louis, the Clemens Mansion on Cass Avenue.

Laura had mentioned nothing to the cabbie about being in a hurry and found herself far from the hotel when they got stuck near a big fire. The cabbie had wanted to show off the glittering stores and homes of the St. Louis rich, but had ended up instead stuck in a line of cars and buggies three blocks long.

A smoking steam pumper raced by, clanging its bells. Laura listened to the rumbling of the wheels and the sharp, quick step of the clomping hoofs. Bright shining harnesses caught the gleam of the sun that poked through the smokey skies.

Laura looked at the traffic jam and tapped the driver. "Is there any other path you can take to get to the hotel?"

The cabbie turned. "Could take you by way of poor town. Don't matter to me."

"Well, I'm kind of in a hurry, so take the shortest way you know."

The cabbie shrugged, backed up, and cut down an alley. "You ain't gonna like this route, lady. This is the poor side of town."

"I'll try to not let it bother me," Laura said, thinking about other things.

About two blocks from the glittering stores the tenements of St. Louis began. Laura sat back quietly, feeling a chill in her soul from the poverty around her. "How long until we get to the hotel?"

"It's just around the corner." Within minutes, they were back to the glittering side of the city. "Here's the Ritz."

Laura tipped the cabbie and let the bellman take her bag to

the front desk. "Hello, Madam," said the spiffy desk clerk with the pencil-thin moustache. "Your name please?"

"Wilder, Mrs. Laura Ingalls Wilder."

"Very good, Mrs. Wilder," he said, looking through a stack of cards, thinking, *And here's the queen of the Ozarks herself.*

"It might be under *The Mansfield Monitor*. I'm here to cover the World's Fair."

"Uh-huh, very good. Here it is," he said, showing the card, and winking at her. " 'Mrs. Laura Ingalls Wilder, honeymoon suite.' "

"Honeymoon suite? Let me see that."

He handed her the card and winked again. "Yes indeed, you've got the special lovers' room."

"I do?" she said with a perplexed look on her face. "What for?"

"Oh, you know," he smiled.

"No, I don't know!" she exclaimed. "What am I going to do in the special lovers' room?"

These people really are backward, the desk clerk thought. "Just whatever comes naturally," he said, winking twice.

"Is there something wrong with your eye?" she asked. She looked at the check-in card, and said, "There must be some mistake."

"No mistake, Mrs. Wilder. This is the requested room."

"I hope this is not Andrew Summers's idea of a joke," she said, getting hot under the collar.

"What?" the desk clerk asked.

"Oh, nothing. Look, I don't need the honeymoon suite by myself. Book me into another room."

He shook his head. "Sorry, madam, the hotel is completely booked up. As a matter of fact, we're overbooked."

"Is there another hotel nearby?"

The desk clerk sighed. "Every hotel for ten miles around is booked. Must be a hundred thousand people here for the fair."

Laura sighed. "I guess I have no choice."

"Unless you want to camp out with the immigrants out by the river," he replied.

"I've had my fill of camping crossing the prairie in a wagon," she said under her breath.

I bet you have, the desk clerk thought. "You'll love the room. It's got a large bed, with soft silk sheets and a French bathtub that two can stretch out in—"

She cut him off. "It sounds wonderful, give me the key, please."

He signaled the bellman. "Take Mrs. Wilder to the honeymoon suite."

The bellhop smiled and winked. "Follow me," he said as he carried her bags toward the elevator.

When the elevator door opened, the bellman said, "Top floor, honeymoon suite."

The old elevator man winked at her. *The whole town must have eye trouble,* Laura thought.

On the top floor, the bellhop led her to the door. From behind them a voice called out, "Excuse me, please."

Laura turned and stepped out of the way as a large arrangement of flowers and a chilled bottle of champagne was brought to the door by a boy from room service.

"Who are these for?" Laura asked. "This is my room. I didn't order these."

Before anybody could answer, the door opened slowly. "I did," Manly said quietly with a grin on his face.

"Manly! What on earth . . ."

He just stood there smiling, looking into her eyes. The room service boy pushed the cart in, put the flowers and champagne down, and accepted the dollar from Manly's hand. He left, winking at Laura, who stood shaking her head and smiling at Manly.

"Honeymoon suite. Manly I didn't know anything about this."

The bellman quietly slipped away, not seeing the dollar tip in Manly's hand.

Laura was overwhelmed. Manly kissed her, then whispered, "This is our big city honeymoon, Laura. I told you I'd keep my promise."

Laura reached out to squeeze his hand and felt the dollar. "What's the dollar for?"

Manly looked down and laughed. "Seems that you got to give everyone 'round here a buck to get somethin' done. Give it to me," he said, taking it from her hand and wrapping his arms around her. "I love you Laura Ingalls Wilder," he whispered, and kissed her like she was still his teenage bride back in the Dakotas.

"Oh, Manly you've gone to all this trouble."

"It was no trouble at all. It's something I should have done for you a long time ago," he said, kicking the door shut.

Laura didn't know what to say. So she let herself drift into the arms of the man who could keep her safe and warm against the unknowns of tomorrow.

"I love you, Manly," she whispered.

CHAPTER 11

OLD FAITHFUL

Larry sat next to Terry who sat next to Sherry in the three hole privy the local carpenter had made for them. Though indoor plumbing had come to the big cities, it hadn't reached the Younguns' house yet. The kids had named their outhouse "Old Faithful."

Looking outside the outhouse, Larry shook his head sadly. "If only Dangit would learn to shake hands instead of bitin' 'em. We'd win that prize money fursure."

Terry took the slingshot out of his britches and shot at a bird sitting on the pole outside his half-door. "It'll take a miracle for Dangit to win. He's too dumb."

Sherry turned to look at her brothers. "Maybe we could teach Dangit to talk like Beezer does."

Larry spit on the ground. "You make Dangit talk and I'll kiss Missouri Poole."

Terry laughed. "You will? Heck, I'll make him sing Dixie for his supper to see your lips on Missouri!"

"That's how sure I am that we've got a loser on our hands," Larry said sadly.

Terry finished his business and left the outhouse. "Wait

up!" Larry shouted, following quickly behind. Sherry was the last to come out and had to catch up with her brothers. She found them sitting in their bedroom, looking over the book Terry had bought from the Johnson-Smith children's fun catalog.

"Read this," Terry said, handing the book to Sherry.

"Can't read," she said, pushing it back at him. "You read it."

"I'm tired of readin'," he said, handing it to Larry. "You read it."

Larry took it. "Tired of readin' my foot. You can't hardly read at all."

"So what?" Terry said. "I just figured out a way to win fifty bucks, maybe a thousand bucks, and you're gripin' 'bout my readin'? With a thousand bucks I could hire you to read everything and I could just play all day."

"Will somebody please read it to me?" Sherry said, pointing to the book.

Larry sighed. "All right, it says . . ." and he read the cover.

VENTRILOQUISM

**An easy method for learning the art of ventriloquism.
A throughly reliable guide to the art of throwing your voice and vocal mimicry. This booklet contains complete directions, by the aid of which any one can acquire this amusing art.
Learn how to immitate birds and animals, etc. 10 cents**

"I don't get it," said Sherry, shaking her head.

"Look dummy, you remember the summer before last when I threw my voice with the ventrillo I bought to make everyone think Silly Willy Bentley was sayin' goofy things?" said Terry.

"Yeah."

"Well, I've been lookin' through this book, learnin' how to ventriloquist myself. Now, what if I threw my voice to Dangit and made people think we had a talkin' dog?"

Larry looked at the cover again. "It says it tells you how to imitate birds and animals. It doesn't say anythin' about teachin' dogs to talk."

"No, no, no! I'm sayin' that I'll stand near Dangit at the show and throw my voice," Terry said. "People will think we got a rare talkin' dog and we'll win the money hands down fursure!"

Sherry looked at the ad. "It shows a man with a dummy on his lap. It doesn't show a Dangit dog sittin' on his lap."

Terry was at his wit's end. "The dummy is for a stage show."

"What do they do?" she asked.

"Look," he said to her, "come over to the bed and sit on my lap. You be the dummy and I'll be Terry, the world's most famous ventriloquist." He went over and sat on the bed and patted his knee. "Come on over and sit right here."

Sherry reluctantly walked over and sat down. "Why do I have to be the dummy?"

"'Cause that's what you do best. Now be quiet. I'm about to do my act."

"What do I do?" she asked.

"Nothin', just be a dummy. You know all about bein' that."

Larry snickered and watched his squirrely brother begin.

"Now, ladies and gentlemen, let me introduce Dum-Dum the Dummy."

Larry clapped and Sherry turned her head. "I don't like that name!"

"Quiet, dummy!" Terry snapped. "Dummies can't talk unless the ventriloquist does the talkin'. Now where was I? Okay, this is Dum-Dum, the world's dummiest dummy."

He stopped to giggle, trying not to burst out laughing.

Larry was cracking up and Sherry was fuming. Terry continued. "Now, Dum-Dum, I want you to say your name."

He said "Dum-Dum" through the side of his mouth. Sherry shouted out, "My name is Sherry Youngun!"

Terry cuffed her on the back of her head. "Sorry, folks, looks like Dum-Dum has a screw loose or somethin'. Now, Dum-Dum, tell us how you got to be so ugly."

Sherry turned around and bopped Terry in the jaw with her fist and ran from the room crying. Larry shrugged. "Didn't work with her but it might just work with Dangit."

Terry smiled. "Let's get the old ventrillo out and practice."

"Dangit the talkin' dog," Larry said, thinking out loud. "I like it. I like it a whole bunch."

CHAPTER 12

BEST OF MOODS

Laura woke up in the best of moods. The first evening of their honeymoon had been wonderful! They had dressed for dinner—Manly had even worn a coat and tie.

Snuggling back down under the thick comforter, Laura closed her eyes to remember each moment of the evening. They lingered over a candlelight dinner, holding hands like teenagers, and talked about the good times they'd shared.

No talk of losing the farm. No talk of being forced to start again. Just happy talk about Manly following her around De-Smet, love-struck and determined to marry her.

Oh, Manly, what a wonderful evening. It was everything I ever dreamed of having. We're going to make the rest of this honeymoon a special time. Just the two of us. Nothing is going to bother us. We're going to enjoy the Fair and love the time away.

I'll remember forever the words you spoke when you held me like there was no tomorrow. "Laura, I'll love you till the day I die and then on through eternity." On through eternity. Whatever awaits us, we'll be together. I just know it.

Laura thought of the music they heard at dinner. Afterward, they strolled on the veranda and through the flower gardens. Then, without asking, Manly guided her into the dance. "I saw your toes tapping. I know how much you love music."

Under the sheets, Laura's toes were wiggling as her mind replayed the wonderful songs they danced to. Manly, even with his limp, had moved across the floor with the grace of a man who spent his weekends as a dandy. When the band struck up "Meet Me In St. Louis, Louis," Manly did a Mansfield version of the Hoochee Koochee that brought the house down!

Then, during the final slow dance of the evening, Manly kissed Laura under the spotlight. The people at the tables around them could sense that something really special was happening. It was the kind of clear, romantic passion that makes people sigh, wishing that same feeling would come into their loves.

Without a word, he gripped her hand and took her back to their honeymoon suite for a wonderful evening of romance. Somewhere among the flowers, candlelight dinner, dancing, and open embracing, Laura and Manly had rediscovered and rekindled their deep love.

We just needed to get away, to be together, Alone, without children, neighbors, or responsibilities. All we needed was the spark to ignite our love.

"You sure are in a good mood," Manly said, smiling at his wife.

"Oh, Manly, last night was the most wonderful evening of my life! I don't know how you kept the surprise from me." She reached over and hugged him tightly. "I'll love you forever for giving this to me, for my big-city honeymoon."

"You talk too much," he whispered, and pulled up the covers.

CHAPTER 13

MEET ME IN ST. LOUIE

They went by cab to the World's Fair and with Laura's press pass, were able to by-pass the long lines. With her note-pad and pencil at the ready, they toured the extravaganza that had people from all over the country flocking to it.

Everyone seemed to be singing "Meet Me in St. Louis, Louis," and Laura telegraphed this story back to *The Mansfield Monitor* from the press room at the fair:

MEET ME IN ST. LOUIE
By Laura Ingalls Wilder

"Meet me in St. Louis, Louis, Meet me at the fair," are the first lines to the song that all America—and certainly everyone in St. Louis—is singing these days. As I wander through the expositions, shows, midways, and the incredibly flamboyant exhibits that bring the best of the past and the future to life, I am impressed with all that is American.

The age of electricity is upon us. Everything about the Fair is lit up in a dazzling array of lights, flags, and machines."

One of the reporters from *The St. Louis Post-Dispatch* has

written words that have reappeared in virtually every paper in the country. "Sell the cook stove, sell the farm, cash in your burial plot, sell anything. You must see this Fair!"

While I wouldn't go so far as to sell the farm or my grave, I would consider selling my old cook stove and trading it in for one of the many fancy electric gadgets shown here. Ice-cooling machines to keep your house cool during the summer, electric fans, and electric trains.

We women will be in heaven over the promise of a brighter tomorrow through electricity. A banner over the hallway of the Woman's Technology building said it all: "Women as a sex have been liberated." I have to admit, these machines were something else to watch in action, and I'm sure my husband was not pleased with the "wish list" I presented him!

How about automatic dishwashers and clothes-washing machines. Can you imagine having those in Mansfield? Why, you'd probably have to keep your doors locked or charge money, because your laundry room would certainly be the most popular drop-in-and-chat place in the town!

The song continues with the words, "We will dance the Hoochee Koochee, I will be your tootsie wootsie." Dance? The whole Fair is jumping with people doing dances that I've never even heard of. This fair is like a twenty-four-hour-a-day New Year's eve party, with bands of every description playing your every fancy.

If you like the weird and wonderful, then the Fair is for you. I saw a ten-ton block of Canadian cheese, a statue of Venus de Milo made from chocolate, a bigger-than-life statue of President Roosevelt made from dried prunes, and a cake the size of a wagon!

So, meet me in St. Louis, people of Mansfield, and see what the outside world has to offer. Those who are lucky enough to make the trip will never forget it.

CHAPTER 14

MANLY BEAR

Their second day in St. Louis, Laura wanted to visit the midway, which was a combination of Coney Island and County Fair. Every conceivable game, sideshow, and food was played, hawked, and eaten.

Laura wanted stuffed bears, and she insisted that Manly throw darts, bowl balls, and toss rings to win one for her. Though he tried his best, he wasn't winning.

Ding. Laura turned at the sound. "Come on, here's something you can win," she said, taking his hand and dragging him along.

Ding. Manly took a deep breath and blew it out, fluttering his lips. *She wants me to slam the mallet and hit the bell. Now I'm really goin' to look like a fool.*

They found a crowd gathered around the barker. "Two bits a whack. Come on boys, win a bear for your girl." He looked at a beefy weight lifter. "Hey you, muscle head, come on over here and see if you can hit the bell," the barker called out. "Look, it's easy." He laughed and tossed the heavy mallet back over his shoulder, then slammed it down on the pad.

Manly's eyes went up, following the path of the lead weight as it flew up the pole. *Ding.*

"See, it's easy," the barker shouted.

"Laura, come on. I'll toss darts at the target again. I'll win you a stuffed bear this time."

"Oh, Manly, you can use a sledgehammer. Just do your best and ring the bell." She looked into his eyes and kissed his lips. "I really *want* a stuffed bear," she whispered.

Manly shook his head. "Come on, Laura. Why do you want me to make a fool of myself in front of all these folks?"

"Just try it. Come on, please. Just do it for the fun of it."

Manly sighed and looked at the muscled men, sailors, and army boys who had lined up to show off for their girlfriends. The weight lifter tried his best, but the lead weight only went up halfway. Two sailors tried and the crowd laughed when one barely got the weight off the pad.

"Who's next?" the barker shouted. "Just two bits."

"He's next," Laura shouted, waving and pointing to Manly.

"No I ain't," Manly protested, but Laura pushed him forward.

The weight lifter stepped in front of Manly. "I want to try it again," he said, handing the barker a dollar.

"You want change, or do you want four chances?" the barker asked.

"Four chances," the weightlifter said, winking to his shapely girlfriend.

Manly was resigned to the fact that he was going to have to try it, so he carefully watched what the barker was doing. There seemed to be no rhyme or reason for how high the lead weight went. Then Manly saw it. *He's got his foot on some kind of device,* Manly thought, watching the barker quickly step on and off a little pad near the pole. *It's rigged. It's a con.* Manly shook his head.

He turned to tell Laura that there was no reason to even try it, but she was standing by the rail, looking at the bears. "I want that one," she said, pointing to the biggest bear.

"Come on, Laura," he said quietly, "let's go."

"But I want that bear," she said, "and I'll name it . . . Manly Bear."

"Hey, buddy," the barker shouted, "it's your turn."

The weightlifter had not been able to ring the bell and was walking off, shaking his head. "Do it, Manly," Laura said, squeezing his hand. "Win one for me. Win me my Manly Bear."

Manly took a quarter from his pocket and walked over to the barker, who was smiling and shaking his head. "Folks," the barker said, "looks like we got ourselves a string bean."

Unable to hold back a blush, Manly took a deep breath. "Here's your quarter."

"Tell you what skinny, I'm goin' to let you have one whack for free." The barker turned to the crowd. "What do you think, folks? Think I should be charitable and let stringbean here have a free whack?"

The crowd laughed. Manly picked up the sledgehammer and tested the weight. "Too heavy for you, string?" the barker said, laughing to the crowd.

"It'll do," Manly said, eyeing the footpad by the rail.

"How about you using this," the barker said, holding up a little toy hammer. "Think this is too heavy for skinny, folks?" he shouted, working the crowd.

Manly leaned over and whispered into the barker's ear. "I seen that trick footpad you been usin' to cheat folks. Now, my wife wants a stuffed bear and you don't want to go to jail. So take my quarter," he said, putting it into the barker's hands, "and keep away from the cheat pad."

"You gonna turn me in to the cops?"

"Nope," Manly said, putting the sledgehammer on his shoulder.

"You want me to work the pad and let you win?" the barker whispered.

"Nope," Manly said, swinging the sledgehammer for balance. "Just let me try and win it fair and square. Don't want nothin' for free."

"Okay, fire away."

Manly put the sledgehammer on his shoulder and looked up the pole to the bell. It was fifteen feet high. He looked at the pad he had to hit to send up the weight, and gauged how much strength it would take.

With a final look at Laura, he bent back and tossed the sledgehammer forward with all his might. The big hammer went down hard, as hard as Manly had ever hit anything in his life.

When it hit the pad, the whole platform shook and the lead weight flew up the pole like a rocket. All eyes in the crowd were on it as it raced upward toward the bell.

Come on, girl, ring that bell, Manly thought.

Ding. Manly could hardly believe it. He'd hit the bell. The crowd began cheering, and Laura raced forward and hugged him.

"You did it, Manly!"

"Go pick yourself the bear you want," he said, kissing her cheek.

The barker shook his head. "Amazing. Stringbean hit the bell."

"My name's not stringbean," Manly said, handing him the sledgehammer.

"I'll call you anything you want. Heck, even Jack the giant killer, if you don't go tell the cops."

"Just give my wife the bear she wants, and we'll be on our way."

Laura came back with the bear she wanted, and walked off

with Manly like he'd just won the world, single-handedly. "Manly Bear," she smiled, "or should I call him Honeymoon Bear."

Manly smiled. "How about just Bear."

CHAPTER 15

MR. TAO

At the end of the midway was a dime museum that promised oddities from around the world.

"Let's go on in," Manly said.

Laura looked at the pictures of freaks of nature in the window. "Oh, Manly, they look so fake."

"Sign says everything's guaranteed real."

"I don't think I want to go in," she said. "Looking at these pictures makes me sad."

"Come on, I won you that bear. All I'm askin' is that you come on in with me. It'll be fun. Aren't you curious?"

"It just seems so sad that nature can twist itself up this way," she said.

"It'll give me somethin' to tell the boys back at the feed store," Manly said, taking her by the hand.

They paid their two-dime admission and went through the curtain. When her eyes adjusted to the dim light, Laura caught her breath. Shrunken heads, painted skulls, leprechaun's clothes, stuffed two-headed animals, and photos of bizarre-looking people were on display.

Laura went back to the booth and asked, "Is everything here real?"

"Why do you ask?" the ticket seller questioned.

"Because I'm a reporter and might write a story about this."

"I will get the owner."

A few minutes later, an oriental man with two pupils in each eye came up to Laura. He wore a red silk robe with wooden buttons. "My name is Mr. Tao. Are you the reporter?"

"Yes. My name is Laura Ingalls Wilder, and this is my husband, Manly." Manly reached out to shake his hand, but Mr. Tao's hands were held together as he bowed slightly.

"I will guide you through my special world," Mr. Tao said. "Please come with me."

Manly did a double take when he looked closely into the man's face. "You got four pupils!"

"And you have good eyes," Mr. Tao said with a smile.

"My word," Laura said. "Can you see normally?"

"What is normal?" the man replied with a slight bow.

"Two eyes and—"

"Please, before you think you know what normal is, please, come see my collection. I'm sure it will be of great interest to you if you are open-minded about wonders of the universe."

Tao guided them through the strange maze of exhibits. Midgets and dwarfs of all descriptions explained some of the exhibits along the way, and were sometimes there as part of the show themselves.

"Where did you find all these little people?" Laura asked.

"Little people are everywhere," Tao said.

"They look like pygmys," Manly said, smiling at a dwarf with a foot-long beard.

"No, they are not pygmys," Tao said and walked on.

"How do you know that?" Manly asked.

Mr. Tao turned to face Manly. "Would you like to meet one?"

"You know one?"

"I know a lot of people . . . who are different," Mr. Tao said, nodding his head slightly. "There is a special person in the Olympics who you should meet."

"Who?" Laura asked.

"I can't say anymore. I haven't gotten a feeling about you yet," Mr. Tao said, walking off. "Come on, there is more to see."

"Let's see that," Manly said, pointing to the "Mermaid" banner over a closed door.

"Don't be ridiculous," Laura said, scoffing at Manly. But she was intrigued herself. *Mermaid?* she thought.

"You will like it very much," said Tao.

Manly pulled her inside. When he looked behind the curtain, he gasped. "That's awful!"

"If that's a mermaid, I'm the Queen of Sheeba," Laura said, hardly able to look at the huge, bloated, leathery creature.

Mr. Tao smiled. "Not everything in life is as it seems. Primitive sailors who first saw manatees actually thought they were mermaids, much the same way that Columbus's sailors thought whales were sea monsters."

"What's a manatee?" Manly asked.

"It's a creature found in the rivers of Florida," Mr. Tao answered. Tao took them to a stuffed cow with six legs. "This is real, very real."

Manly ran his hand over the mounted cow. "It sure was. How'd you get it?"

The guide smiled. "What are freaks of nature to some people are treasures to others. A cow with six legs is of no use to a farmer, but makes a good exhibit for us."

"Gives me the shivers," Laura whispered, looking at the deformed legs sticking out from the cow's back.

"Ah, but life is full of shivers. How else could we know good from evil and normal from abnormal."

It took Laura a moment, but she was finally able to look directly into the Tao's eyes. He smiled. "You see my point. It took you a while to look me in the face, because I have an extra pupil in each eye."

"I'm sorry, I . . ." Laura stammered.

Tao bowed. "No apology necessary. I am used to being different and feel quite at home here with the supposed abnormal and freaks of nature. My extra eyes have given me the ability to see beyond many things we take for granted."

Manly looked closely. "You mean, you see double out of each of them eyes?"

"Yes,"

"That's really strange," Manly said. "I can't imagine having two eyes in each eye."

The man smiled. "And I can't imagine having just one eye in each eye."

"Good point," Laura replied.

"I like you," Mr. Tao said, looking into Laura's eyes. "I have good feelings for you."

Laura didn't know what to say and just stared for a moment until Tao turned to continue the tour. At the next exhibit, two dwarfs explained the pictures of the tallest man in the world. They placed their tiny feet into his size 21EEE shoes. Manly turned to Tao. "You said pygmys were different."

Tao nodded. "Things different from us always seem odd. It is human nature. Pygmies are normal. They are fully developed small people. Throughout history, there have been dozens of different kinds of people that were not like you two. There have been giants and people like the pygmies who were quite normal because they were never intended to grow bigger."

"Giants?" Manly said.

"In this country, on the coast of what you call Texas, lived a tribe of Indians who were giants. Some of them grew to twelve feet or more."

"I'd run if I saw a twelve-foot man comin' after me with a grudge," Manly said with a laugh.

They passed through a hall of wax figures from history. Manly looked at Hannibal, then turned to Tao. "But he's black."

Mr. Tao smiled. "He was black."

"But the book I seen him in showed him as white."

"History shouldn't be changed to make some people comfortable, should it?" Mr. Tao bowed slightly.

At the end of the exhibit, Laura shook Tao's hand. "Thank you very much, Mr. Tao. I've never seen anything like this in my life."

Manly laughed. "Yeah, seems you got a corner on all the oddballs of the world."

Tao smiled, shaking his head slowly. "You Americans have brought thousands of them to St. Louis for amusement."

"I don't know what you're talking about," Laura said.

Tao bowed. "Tomorrow, thousands of 'different' people are being pitted against each other in a sporting event called Anthropology Day. The people brought here from around the world have been told the games are serious, but the promoters have designed them to amuse the crowd."

"What's the difference between that and what you're doin'?" Manly asked.

Tao looked him directly in the eyes. "I respect that which is different and exhibit it for the sake of knowledge. What they are doing is wrong."

"I haven't heard of this Anthropology Day," Laura said.

Tao took a leaflet from his robe pocket and handed it to her.

COME SEE THE PARADE OF MISFITS!
DON'T MISS THIS ONCE-IN-A-LIFETIME OPPORTUNITY TO LAUGH AT GIANTS AND MIDGETS COMPETING TOGETHER IN SOME OF THE SILLIEST SPORTING EVENTS EVER CREATED!

ANTHROPOLOGY DAY STARTS TOMORROW AT THE OLYMPIC STADIUM GROUNDS

We urge everyone not to miss the special Olympic Anthropology Day games, a delight to young and old alike. We promise you will never again see such a collection of freaks and misfits, anywhere in the world!

"This is what I am talking about," Tao said. "Making fun of people who are different. It is disgusting."

"I don't think I want to see that," Laura said, handing the leaflet back to him.

Mr. Tao closed his eyes and was silent for a moment. "I would like to escort you both there."

"It will make me sad," Laura said.

"No, it will make you a better person . . . if you see the events through my eyes," he said, staring intently with his four pupils.

"When are you going?" Manly asked.

"When you both go tomorrow. Be at the gate tomorrow at noon and I will show you something you will never forget."

"Will we ever get to see a pygmy?" Manly asked.

"Perhaps. If you are lucky."

CHAPTER 16

LOVE LETTER

Rev. Youngun sat there reading the letter from Carla Pobst of Cape Girardeau, Missouri, for the third time.

Dear Thomas:
It was wonderful seeing you when you came to Cape. Though so many things were said, so many things were only hinted at and left unsaid. Perhaps I wasn't prepared for the rush of emotions you created within my heart and soul.

Being a widow and you being a widower, we're supposed to mourn the passing of those we loved. Which we do. But in mourning lost love, we nurture within our hearts the capacity to love again.

While I still miss my beloved who was lost at sea, I know that one day I will have enough strength to fill the emptiness in my heart. And so will you. Perhaps we will be together, and perhaps we won't. But there is no denying the feelings we have for each other.

I am planning to visit Mansfield next Monday and would like to see you again. Let's go on another buggy ride, just the two of us. We can talk and try to start things again, without the specter of the memories I felt in Cape.

With fondest regards,
Carla Pobst

Rev. Youngun sighed deeply. *I've tried to put the visit to Cape Girardeau out of my mind and concentrate on raising my three children. But there's no denying that Carla creeps into my thoughts at the oddest of moments. And just when I thought that I had my heart under control, she writes, out of the blue, that she's coming.*

"Hey, Pa, you ready to take us to the dog show?" Larry shouted down from his room.

Rev. Youngun looked at the clock on the wall. The dog show began in an hour. "I'll drop you off on my way to the church."

CHAPTER 17

THE TALKIN' DOG

The Younguns were all set for the big dog show. They spent the morning trying to groom a reluctant Dangit and were now up in their room, teaching Dangit to sit while Terry practiced throwing his voice.

Larry couldn't believe how well the little ten-cent device worked. He read the description of it again in the Johnson-Smith Catalog for kids:

THROW YOUR VOICE

Into a trunk, under the bed, under a table, back of the door, into a desk at school, or anywhere. You get lots of fun fooling the teacher, policeman, peddlers, and surprise and fool all your friends besides.
THE VENTRILLO
is a little instrument that fits in the mouth out of sight. Cannot be detected.

Terry was standing next to Dangit and talking out of the side of his mouth with the ventrillo. Dangit appeared to be saying to Sherry, "Hey stupid, how'd you get so ugly?"

Sherry looked at Dangit and then to Terry. "You said that! Dangit didn't!"

Larry laughed. "Come on, Sherry. You know it's Terry doin' it."

Terry threw his voice again and Dangit appeared to say, "She's too dumb to know the difference."

Sherry began crying and their father called out from downstairs, "What's goin' on up there?"

Terry clamped his hand on Sherry's mouth. "Nothin', Pa."

Sherry kicked him. "Fibber."

Larry stepped between them. "Shush, or Pa'll be comin' up here."

Sherry shrugged. "Why can't we tell him what we're doin'? He knows we're enterin' Dangit in the dog show this afternoon."

Frowning, Larry said, "Because if we tell him that we're gonna pretend Dangit can talk, then he'll tell us we're doin' somethin' like cheatin'. If we don't tell him, then we don't know for sure whether we're cheatin' or not, so we can just go on and do what we're goin' to do."

Larry beamed like he'd just said the most profound thing in the world. Sherry shook her head. "Cheatin's cheatin'."

Terry put his hand over her mouth again. "Quiet. We may think we know but we really don't know and since we don't know, then we don't know if we're cheatin' or not, right?"

Sherry rolled her eyes and sighed. "Right. Whatever you just said."

Terry went inside the closet and snuck a stick of Wrigley's gum into his mouth, carefully chewing so he wouldn't have to offer his brother or sister any. It had taken practice, but he'd developed the fine art of chewing without anyone knowing he was chewing.

Larry looked at Dangit. Sherry tied a pink ribbon around

his head and put bright red lip color on his face. "He don't look right."

"He looks pretty!" Sherry protested.

Terry snorted. "Dogs ain't supposed to be pretty. I think he looks like a fool. Who'd give a ribbon to a boy dog with girl lip color on?"

"Where'd you get the lip color case anyway?" Larry asked.

"Found it."

"Found it where," Larry said, pushing her for an answer.

"Found it in the ladies' outhouse at church."

Terry snickered. "Why didn't you turn it in? It don't belong to you."

"'Cause I wanted it."

"Ain't a good enough reason," Larry said.

Sherry's eyes welled up. "Terry always says, 'Finders keepers, losers weepers.' "

Terry's eyes went wide. "And you always rat on me. I'm tellin' Pa."

Larry grabbed him as he started out of the room. "If you tell Pa, we'll never get to the dog show in time. She can give it back later. Ain't no one still lookin' for the lip color case anyway."

Terry nodded. "Probably thinks it rolled into the dark hole of no return."

"Right," Larry said. "Now come on. Let's go get our fifty bucks."

The three Younguns took Dangit downstairs and went out to the barn to help their father get the wagon ready. They had Dangit wrapped in an old baby blanket that had belonged to Terry, which wasn't going over well with the former owner.

"Still don't see why Dangit has to use my old blanket," Terry said, grumbling.

Larry laughed. "So what? You don't use it anymore."

Terry looked at Sherry, who was sucking her thumb and

clutching her blankey. "Why couldn't Dangit slobber on hers? It'd be warm from all her huggin' and suckin'." He reached over and pulled on it. "Give him *your* blankey!"

Sherry screamed and their father was startled. He turned. "What's going on back there?"

"Nothin', Pa," they all said in unison.

He looked at Dangit. "I think Dangit looks foolish in the pink ribbon. The judges are going to be scoring on more than looks. Does he know any tricks?"

Larry shrugged. "We tried to teach him to sit but when you say sit he just stands and if you say stand he lies down and if you say—"

Rev. Youngun cut his son off. "I think I get the picture. Perhaps you can just tell them that Dangit is a mystery dog who does what he wants."

Rev. Youngun was not known for his great jokes, and his dry humor usually went above the kids' heads. Behind his back, Terry rolled his eyes and mimicked a silent, mocking laughter, like what his father said was the funniest thing in the world.

Without warning, Rev. Youngun turned around. "What are you doing, Terry, choking?"

Terry quickly straightened up and gulped. "Couldn't hardly stop laughing at your funny jokes, Pa. I *love* your jokes."

Rev. Youngun smiled. "I should do it more often. I don't want you kids growing up thinking that I'm just a serious old bookworm."

They all rolled their eyes as he turned back around. When they neared the town meeting hall where the dog show was to be held, they were struck by the number of cars, buggies, and wagons that lined the streets.

"More cars than Mansfield's got people, ain't they, Pa?" Larry said.

Rev. Youngun nodded. "I've never seen this many cars in Mansfield before."

There was a big banner over the doorway which read, *MANSFIELD DOG SHOW.* Terry shook his head, "These people must love dogs more than fleas do."

Dangit scratched behind his ears and pulled off the ribbon. "Speakin' of fleas," Larry said, "Dangit's got the itchies again."

Sherry tied the ribbon back on and patted him on the head. "Now, you look pretty again."

Larry tapped his father on the shoulder. "Pa, after we win the fifty bucks, maybe you should take some time off. We'll loan you some money."

Rev. Youngun took it as a compliment. "Why, I might just do that, son, thanks."

"Yeah," Terry said, "and when we win that trip to St. Louis next week, you can come with us."

Rev. Youngun didn't want to tell them yet that Carla Pobst was coming for a visit and that he couldn't go to St. Louis or anywhere else next week. But he was sure that there was no chance in the world that Dangit would win, so he decided to say nothing about it right then. Instead he humored his children.

"St. Louis is a big city." he said. "The World's Fair would be a sight to see. It'd be fun to go, wouldn't it?"

"Sure would, Pa," Terry said, hugging his father.

Rev. Youngun halted the wagon at the front entrance. Three well-dressed folks stood in line, holding their primped and pampered little dogs.

Sarah Bently, the sponsor of the show, greeted everyone as they entered. Her son William the third, whom the kids at school called *Silly Willy* because of the "Little Lord Fauntleroy" clothes he wore to school, stood behind her.

Terry snickered. "Look at Silly Willy. His dog looks stupider than he does."

Willy was holding the pink leash to a fluffed-out poddle with ribbons around its ears. Larry made a face. "That thing looks like a white rat covered with glue and cotton."

"Hey, Silly Willy, that's a nice powder puff you're draggin' 'round," Terry shouted.

Sarah Bentley heard it and gave the Younguns a frosty stare. "Good afternoon, Rev. Youngun. Are you coming to watch the show?"

Rev. Youngun tipped his hat. "No, Mrs. Bentley, I'm just dropping my children off. They're entering their dog in your contest."

"Well," Mrs. Bentley said, looking at Dangit with the lip color and ribbon, "this *is* a charity event."

The Younguns didn't catch her meaning and Terry brightened up. "Does that mean you're lettin' Dangit enter free?"

"No," she said, shaking her head, "*everyone* has to pay."

Another well-dressed lady carrying a groomed collie came to the door and was greeted by Mrs. Bentley. Rev. Youngun looked at his three children standing on the sidewalk staring up at him.

"Remember, come right home after the contest."

"Yes, Pa," they all said in unison.

"And no funny business in there, okay?"

"Yes, Pa."

"I'll see you at supper." He looked at Dangit. "And good luck to you, Dangit."

Terry put his wad of gum behind his ear and slipped the ventrillo in his mouth. Dangit turned his head sideways to look at Rev. Youngun and Terry threw his voice. "Thanks, Pa."

Rev. Youngun did a double take and Dangit sat up with his tongue out. Larry gave Terry the "quit it" look and picked up Dangit.

Terry popped the gum back in and smiled. "Thanks, Pa. We'll see you at supper." He started inside. "Come on, let's go get our fifty bucks."

The children waved to their father and as they walked in. Larry whispered, "That was pretty durn dumb."

Terry shrugged. "Couldn't help it. I needed the practice."

CHAPTER 18

THE MANSFIELD DOG SHOW

Willy watched the Younguns walk up. *They're always up to something,* he thought. He stuck his hand out. "That'll be one dollar."

"This'll be one dollar," Terry said, making a fist.

Willy made a face. "One dollar. My mom says everyone pays."

Larry shook his head. "Come on, Willy, be a pal and let us in."

"Can't. My mom said everyone has to pay one dollar."

Terry got up close, winked, and whispered, "Come over here."

He took Willy by the hand and pulled him into the corner. The Younguns crowded against Willy.

Terry looked Willy in the eyes. "Let us in and I'll give you this famous Indian arrowhead," he said, pulling out the rock he'd found at the creek.

Willy looked around and then stared at the rock. "Don't look like an arrowhead. Kind of chipped up, ain't it?"

Terry nodded. "Took a lot of beatin' when it killed . . . him."

Larry rolled his eyes behind Willy's back, knowing that Terry was tellin' a fibber again. Sherry stood transfixed, believing every word.

"Killed who?" Willy whispered, moving closer.

"Custer," Terry said, very matter-of-factly.

"You mean . . . ?"

"I do mean. None other than General Custer, who gave his life at the Battle of Little Shoe Horn."

Willy raised his eyes and Larry corrected his brother. "He means the Battle of Little Big Horn."

"That's right," Terry said, not missing a beat. "This was pulled from Custer's heart by Pocahontas, the squaw bride of Geronimo, the Indian who killed him."

Willy was impressed. "You mean you'll give me that if I let you sneak in?" All three Younguns shook their heads up and down. "Okay," Willy said, looking around. He didn't see Terry wink at Larry. "Just go on in and take box number thirteen." He grabbed the famous arrowhead and stuck it in his pocket.

Sherry and Terry started forward, but Larry stopped them. "Can't."

Terry, thinking his brother had another untimely burst of conscience, grabbed his sleeve. "Oh, yes, we can!"

"Can't take booth thirteen. That's an unlucky number."

Willy was exasperated. His mother called out to him, "William, I need your help at the door."

"Be right there, Mother." He turned back to the Younguns. "Then take box thirty-nine. Just get in there before my mother finds out."

Larry grabbed the tag and the Younguns scooted through the door. Willy walked back and stood beside his mother.

She looked at him and said, "Were those Youngun children bothering you, son?"

"No, they just wanted to talk about history and things."

"That's good, son," she said without looking. "I just didn't want them trying to talk you into something. That little red-headed one is a rascal."

Inside, the large meeting hall was controlled chaos. Dogs barked, owners tried to hush them, and people who should have known better fawned over their dogs like they were children.

"Sweetums, let Daddy brush your hair," a butterball of a man said to his cocker spaniel with ribbons.

Larry looked at Terry. "That man's an idiot callin' himself *Daddy* to a dog."

Terry shrugged. "There are a lot of ugly kids in this world. Maybe he needs glasses and thinks that dog's his kid."

A big woman with enough bird feathers on her hat to fly pushed past them, then stopped to talk to another woman. She was carrying a hairball with four clipped, pampered paws.

Sherry giggled. "Looked like a bunch of hair with toes."

Mr. Chan came up to chat, carrying his wrinkled Shar-Pei named Noodles. "You're entering Dangit?"

"If you can enter Noodles, we can enter Dangit," Larry said defensively.

Terry didn't want to talk to Mr. Chan because he was curious about the hairy thing in the feather woman's arms. So he sneaked up behind the lady and peered at the little ball of fur.

"Poor fella, you can't see," he whispered to the dog, pushing back the dog's hair. "Pa said it ain't good to have hair hangin' in your eyes."

Without the woman's noticing, he took the wad of gum from his mouth and squished it into the hair above the dog's eyes. Terry stood back and admired his work and the dog's blinking, bugged-out eyes. "Now you can see, can't you fella," he said, backing toward Larry.

The woman spun the dog around. "I have to brush my Puffy Baby." She took out a pink brush from her purse and began combing until she got it stuck in the mess Terry had made. "Gum! Who put gum in my Puffy Baby's hair?"

"What's all the commotion about?" Larry asked.

"Somethin' 'bout her dog chewin' gum or somethin'," Terry said, shrugging his shoulders.

Larry whistled. "Dog chewin' gum. Man, Dangit does have some competition in this show."

They found box number thirty-nine. Terry looked around, worrying that someone might see his mouth move when he threw his voice. "Maybe I should hide under the box and throw my voice."

"How you gonna get under it without anyone seein' you?"

Terry looked around. "Don't know, got any ideas?"

Sherry brightened with an idea. "Let's take the box out back. You can get in out there."

Terry had to admit it *was* a good idea. He picked up the box and started for the back door. "Come on, we got to hurry."

Once outside, they waited until the coast was clear and then Terry crawled under the box. Larry looked around and then talked to the box. "Are you okay under there?"

"Can't see."

"Let me poke an eyehole," Larry said, pushing on a knothole.

"Hey, watch it. You're pokin' my eye!"

"Sorry."

"I'm okay, let's go back in," Terry said. He stood up under the box and began to walk back to the meeting hall.

"Stop, stop," Larry said, but it was too late. The back door opened and a man came out. It was Four-Eyes Johnson, the desk clerk at the Mansfield Hotel who wore thick, thick glasses.

"Hello, Mr. Johnson," Larry said, pushing the box back down.

"Watch it!" Terry whispered.

Four-Eyes peered at the kids. "Who are you children?"

"We're the Younguns," Sherry said.

"Oh, Rev. Youngun's children. Good to see you, good to see you." He looked at them closely. "Where's the redhead?"

"Oh," Larry said, kicking his toe behind his other leg. "He's close behind somewhere."

"Close behind to your behind," Terry said from under the box.

Four-Eyes blinked and turned his head. "Who said that?"

Larry and Sherry just shrugged.

Four-Eyes looked at the box and said, "What a convenient place to put a chair. I do need a rest." He sat down on it and began humming.

Terry was fit to be tied. "Get off me!" he shouted.

Four-Eyes stopped humming. "What did you say?" he asked Larry.

"I didn't say—"

Terry shouted from under the box again. "Get up! Get off me!"

Four-Eyes stood up. "It sounded like the box was talkin'!" He turned to Larry. "Did you hear it?"

Larry shrugged. "Didn't hear nothin'. Maybe it was your stomach gurglin' or somethin'."

"Well," Four-Eyes said, "guess I'm hearin' things. Maybe I better sit back down and rest."

At that exact moment, Terry stood up, and moved the box forward. Four-Eyes fell on the ground!

"Who moved the box?" Four-Eyes shouted out, trying to adjust his glasses.

"Not me," Larry and Sherry said in unison.

"Funny," Four-Eyes said, getting up and dusting himself off, "I could have sworn it was right here."

Larry turned to Sherry. "You bring Dangit. I'll bring the

box. We got to go. Nice seein' you Four . . . er, Mr. Johnson."

Larry picked up one end of the box and dragged it into the meeting hall. "You almost got us caught," he said to the box.

Terry stuck his tongue out through the eye hole. "You wouldn't want Four-Eyes sittin' on your head either."

Maurice and Eulla Mae Springer walked up and down the aisles, admiring the various dogs. When Maurice noticed Larry talking to the box, he excused himself from Eulla Mae and went over to the Younguns. "What you talkin' to the box for?"

Larry stopped talking and looked up. "Oh, er, hi, Mr. Springer."

"Hi. I asked you why you were talkin' to the box?"

"Talkin' to the box? I . . . I . . ." Larry stammered.

"Hi, Mr. Springer," Terry said without thinking from inside the box.

"Terry, is that you Terry. Where are you?"

"I'm in here."

Maurice peered at the box. "In the box?"

Terry stuck his finger through the eye hole. Maurice didn't know what to do, so he put his hand out and shook Terry's finger.

"People see me shakin' hands with a box, they'll have me committed for sure." He turned to Larry, "What you kids got goin' on?"

"Nothin', Mr. Springer," they all said in unison.

"Nothin' my foot! Ain't no other reason you got that brother of yours in the box unless he's up to no good." He tapped on the box. "Terry, you come out of there."

"We're just playin' hide-n-go-seek," Terry said, with one eye looking out.

From the front of the room, Mrs. Bentley shouted into a

megaphone, "Ladies and Gentlemen, we're about to begin this year's Mansfield Dog Show. Contestants, take your places."

"Got to go," Larry said, staggering off with the box in tow.

Maurice watched them go. "They're up to no, no good, that's for sure," he mumbled, shaking his head.

"What did you say?" Eulla Mae asked, walking up next to him.

"Oh, nothin'. Just talkin' to a box."

Eulla Mae just stared at him like he had bumped his head. "You feelin' all right? Maybe you better sit down . . . I'll go get you a cold drink," she said, walking off.

Larry sat the box down at space thirty-nine. On the right was a drooling bulldog, on the left a prissy Yorkshire Terrier. Sherry looked at the bulldog and shook her head.

The dog's owner tapped her shoulder. "What you shakin' your head for, kid?"

"Ain't right," she said, looking at the drool dripping from the dog's mouth.

"What ain't right?"

"Puttin' an old dog in the show. Poor old thing ought to be in a rest home."

"What?" the man said, protesting. "This is a puppy."

Sherry shook her head back and forth. "Dog looks sick to me."

"What did she say?"

"Oh, nothin'," Larry said, pulling Sherry back.

Inside the box, Terry had poked an eye hole on each side to give him clear vision all around. He wanted to spy on people but soon bored of the game.

"Think I'll practice," me mumbled to himself.

He threw his voice to the bulldog who was lookin' into his owner's face. The dog seemed to say, "Your breath stinks." The man snapped back and looked around, wondering if he was going crazy.

The owner of the Yorkshire was a very prim and proper man. Terry tossed his voice into the Yorkshire's mouth as his owner nuzzled him. "Hey, your fly's open."

The man looked down and then all around. "Who said that?" The man grabbed a fan and waved it around his head. "Oh, Blossom," he said to his dog, "I hope Daddy's not getting sick again."

Larry saw it all and tapped on the box. "Quiet in there."

Terry wiggled his finger out of the front eye hole with a "come down here" motion. Larry bent over and Terry whispered, "Shut up or I'm goin' home and we don't get our fifty bucks."

"Okay, okay," Larry relented. "But quit tossin' your voice. Save it for the judges."

"I'm thirsty," Terry moaned. "It's hot in here!"

"Hold on, I'll get you somethin'." Larry walked over and bought a nickel Coke and brought it back. "Here," he said, sticking the neck through the front eye hole, "sip on this."

Maurice stood one aisle over, eyeing the Younguns, watching the bottle empty itself into the box. *I know they're up to somethin'. I just know it,* he thought.

Sarah Bentley followed the judges around as dog after dog was observed. Some of the dogs barked and tried to get off their boxes, which immediately disqualified them. Others, did what they were supposed to do. Dangit just laid on the box and went to sleep with his paws over his ears.

"Dangit's asleep," Sherry said to Larry.

"That's 'bout the only trick he does well," Larry shrugged.

When the judges got to the Yorkshire, his owner was very nervous. But Blossom warmed the hearts of the judges. As they moved on, the Yorkshire's owner fawned all over him. "Oh, Blossom, you were wonderful, simply wonderful!"

Larry rolled his eyes, then straightened up as the judges

lined up in front of Dangit. "Wake up, Dangit," he whispered. Dangit responded by raising one ear and opening one eye.

"What have we here?" asked the kindly old judge.

The younger judge next to him remarked, "Looks like a rare mutt." Sarah Bentley and the third, tall, skinny judge giggled.

Sherry fumed. "That weren't nice!"

"Ah-hem," the kindly judge said, clearing his throat and poking the wise-mouthed judge. "He was only kidding."

"And what is your dog's name?" the third judge asked.

"Dangit," said Larry.

"And what makes Dangit special?" the kindly judge asked, acutely aware that the other two judges wanted to move on.

"Ask him a question," Sherry smiled.

Maurice moved closer, mumbling to himself, "Ask Dangit a question? I should have known it. They *are* up to somethin'."

The kindly old judge humored her. "Okay, what do you think of Mrs. Bentley's new dress?"

Sarah Bentley blushed and spun around, so everyone could admire her dress. "Straight from Paris," she said.

Dangit cocked his head to the judge and opened his mouth, ever so slightly. "Paris, Tennessee, you mean, chunky!"

Mrs. Bentley stopped spinning and gasped. The kindly judge smiled and pulled on his ear. "Maybe I'm hearing things. Did that dog just speak?"

Dangit sat up and appeared to say, "You need a hearin' aid or somethin'?"

The judge looked at Sherry. "Can I ask Dangit to do something?"

"Sure!" said Sherry loudly. "Dangit's the only talkin' dog in the world."

Larry looked around. He could hear the words "talkin' dog?" pass from lips to lips all around them. Like spontaneous combustion, people began pressing toward Dangit.

"Okay," the judge said. "Simon says, bark."

Dangit cocked his head and appeared to say, "Simon says go brush your teeth. Your breath stinks!"

The whole crowd broke up with laughter and a ripple of applause broke out. "How did you train your dog to talk?" the snooty judge asked.

Larry shrugged. "I guess when we paper trained him, he must have read 'em first."

The crowd really laughed at that, but Sarah Bentley was fit to be tied. "How can a dog talk? What is he, part parrot?"

"Pretty good trick, I'd say," the third judge nodded.

Sarah Bentley fumed and looked Dangit in the face. "I think there's somethin' goin' on here," she said, looking at Larry and Sherry. "Where's the redhead?"

"Ah . . . er. . . ." Larry stammered, "he got kinda boxed in."

Mrs. Bentley interrupted him. "I think this is a trick!"

Dangit turned his head and wagged his tail. "You got crow's feet and a double chin!"

Sarah Bentley's eyebrows arched! She spun around and stormed off. The old judge smiled. "This dog is amazing, simply amazing."

Maurice pushed through the crowd. Everyone was trying to ask Dangit questions at the same time. He pulled Larry aside and said, "You better say Dangit's tired before Terry goes crazy on you."

Larry turned to hear Terry throw his voice, "Give me money. Give me dollar bills." Larry nodded to Maurice. "You're right, Mr. Springer."

He stepped back to the box just as Dangit appeared to be saying to an elderly man, "Give me a hunnert bucks and I'll make you young again."

Larry closed his eyes and leaned down next to the box. "Quiet. You're gettin' out of hand."

Maurice saw a reporter from *The St. Louis Post-Dispatch* walking toward them, so he leaned next to the box. "Terry Youngun, *I know* you're in there and *I know* that Dangit ain't doin' the talkin'. Now you either hush up or I'm goin' to turn this box upside down. You understand?"

"Yes, Mr. Springer."

The reporter, accompanied by a lady friend, turned to her and laughed. "These rubes will believe anything."

The lady friend protested. "But I heard the dog talk."

"And bears fly," he said, shaking his head. "These kids just pulled the rug over the rubes' heads." He turned and walked toward Dangit.

"Where you going?" she called out.

"To talk to the dog. The people of St. Louis will get a real laugh out of this one!" When he got in front of Larry, he smiled, trying to look sincere. "Let's hear the talkin' dog."

"Dangit's tired," Larry said.

"Just one word," the reporter whispered, looking at Dangit. "Bowser, you got a statement for the press?" he said, snapping a picture of the group.

Dangit turned his head. "Put a buck in the box."

The reporter laughed. "Just like a politician! Okay, here's a buck," he said, sticking it into the hole. He blinked as the dollar was pulled in.

Dangit just sat there while the reporter waited. Finally, he said, "I gave you a buck, now say something!"

Maurice whispered to Larry, "Get Dangit outta here—fast." Turning to the reporter, Maurice said, "Dangit's tired and don't want to be interviewed just now. Maybe later, after he's won the contest."

"Are you his manager or somethin'?" the reporter asked.

"Naw, just his . . . just his . . ."

Sherry grabbed the reporter's sleeve. "Mr. Springer taught Dangit everythin' he knows."

"You did, did you? Is that Springer or Singer?"

"It's Springer and—"

"And I paid a buck to hear that mutt speak, now say somethin'," he said, kneeling beside the box. Terry reached out and pinched his arm. "Ow!" the reported cried out. "Dangit, that hurts."

Dangit cocked his head to the misuse of his name and Terry threw his voice one more time. "You're history now!"

The reporter didn't understand but Dangit explained it to him by jumping off the box and ripping off his pants' cuff. Larry pulled Dangit off and ran for the back door. Sherry followed closely behind,

"Hey wait for me!" Terry shouted, leaving Maurice to deal with the reporter and his ripped pants' leg. In all the confusion, no one seemed to notice the box walking across the room.

Outside, Terry got out and put the ventrillo in his pocket. The door swung open and the kindly judge came out. "I don't know what you kids did, but it was more original than anything I've ever seen at one of these stuffy dog shows."

"Thanks, Mr. Judge," Larry said.

"You kids better get back inside."

"Are we in trouble?" Sherry asked quietly.

"In trouble? Why, heavens no! Just come on back in."

Rev. Youngun had finished all his church work. He had called Carla Pobst long distance from the general store, and told her that he'd meet the noon train on Monday. Just the day after the next. He didn't know what to think, but was in such a good mood, he decided to stop by the dog show.

I bet the kids are pretty upset, realizing they're not going to win, he thought. He parked the wagon on the side of the town meeting hall and walked in, just as they were announcing the winner.

The kindly judge lifted up his hands for silence. "This is the moment you've all been waiting for."

Rev. Youngun saw Maurice and Eulla Mae and approached them. Eulla Mae looked up and smiled. "How'd you keep it a secret?"

"Keep what secret?" Rev. Youngun asked. "What are you—"

The judge cut him off. "Quiet everyone. It's time to announce the winner, though this year there's no real question. Coming in third, is Mr. Bedal's French poodle." People nodded and clapped as Lafayette Bedal walked on stage with his poodle.

"Bon jour, merci," he said as he waved to the crowd.

Rev. Youngun pressed Maurice for an answer. "What secret?"

"You wouldn't believe me so you just listen."

"Coming in number two," shouted the judge, "is Mr. Chan's wrinkly Shar-Pei, Noodles." Someone had managed to sneak a Chinese gong in, and hit it at that moment to honor Chan. He bowed to the crowd and carried off the second place trophy.

The judge raised his hands again. "And the winner of the 1906 Mansfield Dog Show is . . ." he pointed his finger to a drummer from the county band who began a ragged drum roll. "And the winner is . . . Dangit the talking wonder dog!"

The crowd began cheering as the three Younguns marched on stage to get their trophy, which was bigger than they were. Larry carried Dangit and Terry slipped the ventrillo into his mouth. Rev. Youngun was speechless.

Signaling for quiet, the judge patted them on the head. "This dog of yours is amazing, kids, simply amazing. This is history in the making." He took Dangit's paw and shook it.

"Congratulations, Dangit. Do you have anything to say to the crowd?"

Larry tickled Dangit, to get his mouth open. Terry tossed his voice, "Give me the fifty bucks!"

The crowd roared with laughter. Sarah Bentley was still fuming and when she saw Rev. Youngun out in the crowd, she whispered into the judge's ear, pointing to Rev. Youngun. He was slack-jawed, staring at Maurice.

Maurice shrugged. "I don't know what to say."

The judge shouted out, "Rev. Youngun, come on up here with your kids. You've got to be mighty proud!"

Sherry's mouth dropped. Larry looked at Terry who gulped and palmed the ventrillo out of his mouth and into his pocket. People in the audience pushed Rev. Youngun forward, slapping him on the back in a friendly way. When he got to the edge of the stage, he locked eyes with his children, giving them his best "you're going to get it" stare.

The judge pulled Rev. Youngun up. "I bet these kids are a chip off the old block, aren't they Rev. Youngun?"

Terry, seeing the fix his father was in, stepped forward. "We sure are and we're proud of it."

Larry added, "He never beats us or yells at us. He gives us nothin' but love."

"Yeah," said Sherry, grabbing onto his leg. "He's the bestest daddy in the whole world."

Larry said to the crowd, "Pa's speechless because he knows how much the fifty bucks is going to help the poor children of the community."

Rev. Youngun looked at Larry. He knew that Larry was *cutting a deal,* trying to worm out of the mess they were in. He didn't know how they'd pulled it off, but he would find out later.

The judge held up the crisp, new, fifty-dollar bill. "And who's going to take this home along with the trophy?"

Terry snatched it. "I'm goin' to give it to the poorest child I know. Thank you."

Maurice came to the edge of the stage and said, "Hand me Dangit. It's time for you folks to get this wonder dog home."

Rev. Youngun reached for the bill, but the judge stopped him. "And here's your train passes to St. Louis and free room and board at the West Side Hotel." He looked at the kids. "You all are going to the World's Fair!"

While the audience cheered, the judge whispered into Rev. Youngun's ear, "I don't know how your kids did it, but that's the neatest trick I've ever seen. That red-haired one's a great ventriloquist!"

Outside the building, Rev. Youngun assembled his children. "I want to know what you did." The three of them stood there and didn't speak.

Sherry clutched the trophy. "Don't take it from us, Pa."

Rev. Youngun was fuming. "Talking dog? How could you do something like that?"

"Sorry, Pa," they all said in unison.

"Can we keep the money?" Terry whispered.

"Do you think you deserve it?"

Terry thought for a moment. "Yup. They didn't say nothin' 'bout no ventrilloin' or nothin'. And we didn't have enough money to get Dangit's hair all fluffed up."

Rev. Youngun shook his head. "Dangit doesn't even have any hair."

"That's why we couldn't fluff it out then," Terry said with a shrug.

"What about the trip to St. Louis, Pa? You promised to go if we won."

"I did not." Then he realized that he probably had. *What am I going to do?*

"We got train tickets and a free hotel and everythin', Pa," Larry pleaded. *"We got to go."*

"And trick more people?"

"No, Pa, no!" Terry said. "We'll do it fair and square, honest."

Maurice came out laughing. "Land's sake, you had them goin' in there. Guess they all thought you were some vaudeville act or somethin'."

"I might need to look for that kind of job if word of this gets out," Rev. Youngun said. "Talkin' dog? I can hear them at the next church conference now."

"Can you take us to St. Louis, Pa?" Sherry asked.

"I can't . . . I . . ."

"You what?" Larry asked.

"I've got a visitor coming."

"Visitor? Who?" Terry asked loudly. "Not Uncle Cletus again!"

"Not Aunt Myrtle," Sherry said, moaning even louder.

"No, no." Rev. Youngun looked at Maurice for a brief moment, then back to the kids' faces. "You remember the widow, Carla Pobst, from Cape Girardeau?"

"Oh, no!" Terry shouted. "I thought you were through with the widow woman!"

"We're just friends."

"She wants to be our momma," Sherry said, cutting him off.

"No, but she's comin' and . . . that's why I can't go."

Maurice, who wanted to go see the World's Fair, looked at the train tickets and hotel pass. "I'll take 'em."

Rev. Youngun stopped. "You will?"

"Sure 'nough. I'll take 'em up on the train and bring 'em back after the contest. Heck, they just might win the thousand-dollar prize at the St. Louis contest."

Rev. Youngun looked at Maurice. "Do you know what you're getting yourself into?"

Maurice leaned over and whispered, "I know I'm gettin' you off the hook."

Rev. Youngun saw it as a possible solution. "I'll agree on one condition. No more tricks. Let Dangit win or lose on his own merits."

"Yes, Pa," they all said in unison, but they weren't really paying attention to what he said.

As the kids ran to the wagon, screaming with delight, Maurice put his hand on Rev. Youngun's shoulder. "You can't get that monkey business off your mind, can ya'?"

Rev. Youngun blushed. "We're just friends."

Maurice laughed, cutting him off. "I'm takin' the mice away so the cat can play!"

CHAPTER 19

THE THIRD OLYMPICS

Andrew Jackson Summer's reporter friend, Jack Dunning, came by the hotel to give Laura the background on the problems the Olympics promoters were facing. Manly decided to sit with them in the lobby, pretending to be interested in the games, but really just to keep his eye on Dunning. He didn't trust newspaper men.

"The Third Olympic Games got off to a real bad start," he said to Laura in the lobby.

"What's happened?" she asked.

Dunning shook his head. "Only twelve countries and six hundred athletes have come to take part in the games."

"That doesn't sound like much of an international event."

"It's not," Dunning said, shaking his head. "With the fight between Chicago and St. Louis over which city would get the Olympics, and President Roosevelt stepping in to make the choice, Olympics President Pierre de Coubertin announced his refusal to come. He called the games a farce."

Laura and Manly listened attentively as Dunning rattled off all the problems. European athletes claimed it was too expensive to come; news of war in the Far East was keeping others away; the organizers were short of money. There seemed no end to the troubles.

"What's going to happen?" Laura asked.

"The games have turned into just a sideshow to the World's Fair."

"Where are they being held?" Manly asked.

"They're scattered all around. Without funds, no real planning went into preparing Olympic facilities. They didn't even build the stadium like they promised."

"Then how are they holding the games?" Laura asked.

"Most of the contests are being held on the Washington University campus. The runners have been using a one-third mile oval track and the marathon runners have literally risked their lives running down busy streets."

"That's awful," Laura said.

Dunning frowned. "And that's not the worst of it," he said. "They built an artificial lake for the swimming events which has turned into one big disaster. The starting platform sank under the weight of the swimmers, so they've been forced to begin their races standing in water up to their knees."

"No records are going to be set that way," Manly said.

"We're going over there in the morning," Laura told Dunning.

"Be careful what you eat," Dunning said seriously. "The Fair's food is bad enough, but it's criminal what they're feeding the athletes."

"Criminal?" Laura asked.

Dunning nodded. "Without money, the organizers could only afford to buy old buffalo meat. The rest is donated food. Some of the athletes are so hungry, I've seen them begging for handouts from the crowds."

"What are the promoters going to do? Shut down the games?" Laura asked.

"They're trying a publicity stunt tomorrow. Calling it Anthropology Day. They're hoping the publicity will bring paying crowds so they can break even."

"That's where we're going tommorrow," Laura said.

"You and Alice Roosevelt," Dunning said.

"Alice Roosevelt?" Manly said. "Is the president's daughter coming?"

"The President wants her to crown the winners of the Anthropology Day events."

"Why would he send her?" Laura asked.

"Votes," Dunning said, shaking his head.

CHAPTER 20

THE PRESIDENT'S DAUGHTER

Alice Roosevelt Longworth, daughter of President Teddy Roosevelt, was called the woman of the decade. She was America's real-life Gibson Girl, living the life of wealth, parties, and lavish gifts bestowed upon her from leaders around the world.

The *Journal des Debats* of Paris said that in the fifteen months they followed her, she had attended over four hundred dinners, nearly the same number of balls, and at least three hundred lavish parties. It was written that, "she danced till dawn with the men who had least reason to expect the honor and laughingly disappointed those who had counted on her."

America was without royalty but seemed to find a touch of it in Alice. Millions of baby girls had been named for her during that decade, and "Alice Blue" became an accepted color because of the color of gowns she favored. Her picture could be found on the covers of magazines on newsstands around the world, and her father made a point of saying that while he might be able to control Congress, he couldn't control his daughter. She was strong willed and spoke her mind, no matter what the occasion.

Alice was exceptionally pretty. But in an age when women were still to be seen and not heard, Alice was heard. She smoked in public, fired pistols in the air for excitement, and was known to jump into swimming pools, fully clothed, to liven up a dull party.

Alice had the world at her fingertips. She played poker at Capitol Hill, and danced the hula in Hawaii. She was the guest of the Empress of China at the Imperial Palace in Peking. The four-feet-tall Sultan of Sula wanted to make the "American Princess" wife number seven, but Alice later told the press, "I would have considered it, but he was a bit short for me."

She had brought her black dog—a gift from the Empress of China—to compete as an honorary entrant in the St. Louis Dog Show and under pressure from her father, had agreed to preside over some of the Olympic events.

When she got to St. Louis and read the literature on the Anthropology Day events, she was outraged and telegraphed her father:

Dear Father President:
I have met the organizers of the Anthropology Day Events and don't like them. They told you this was a sporting event for all people from around the world. Instead, it is a cruel joke, a publicity trick to sell tickets to their failing Olympics.
They are calling the entrants "misfits" when in fact, it is the promoters and organizers who are the misfits. I want to come home.

Alice

President Roosevelt had fought to put the olympics in St. Louis and was outraged that Olympic Committee President

Coubertin refused to come. He needed his daughter to publicize the events. So, while he watched war brew in Asia, a pending revolution in Russia, and a hostile Congress, he telegraphed her back:

Dear First Daughter Alice:
Use your charm and pursasion to make the best of it. Perhaps you can make the organizers see the light. If you can't, I'm sure there are enough parties and balls to occupy your time.

Father

Alice turned at the knock on her hotel door. "Yes?" The mayor of St. Louis had assigned his top aide to watch over the President's daughter. He stuck his head in.

"I've got your itinerary for the day. Would you like to review it?"

Alice nodded and read the paper. She was to first take a tour through the fashionable sections of St. Louis, have tea with one of the town's elite, then go to the Olympic Village and tour the villages representing the lifestyles of the various entrants in the Anthropology Day events.

"Is there anything fun to see?" said Alice, still thinking about the telegram.

"Oh yes, you're going to love the Fair and Olympics."

"I mean on the way to the events."

The aide thought for a moment. "Would you like to see the Taj Majhal?"

"I've seen it."

The aide laughed. "No, I mean the Taj Majhal of Saint Louis."

"Is it a replica?"

"No, but it's the nickname we've given the Clemens Mansion on Cass Avenue. Clemens was a cousin of Mark Twain. He used to stay there a lot. And General Danny Custer stayed there on his trip out west to the Battle of Little Big Horn. Kind of last supper you might call it."

"That sounds a bit more interesting since I like Mark Twain's writing. Let's get this over with," she said, stuffing the telegram into her purse. She was escorted to the elevator by six members of the St. Louis police honor guard who were assigned to her service and protection for the entire trip.

In the lobby of the Ritz, she was greeted with a blaze of camera flashes and reporter's questions. "Hey, Alice," shouted Jack Dunning, "I hear you're excited about judging the freak show. Can that be true?"

"This is something my father asked me to do. Shouldn't daughters do what their fathers ask them?" she said, batting her eyes.

"But you're married to Congressman Nicholas Longworth, Speaker of the House," Dunning shot back.

Alice smiled. "My husband may be the Speaker, but my father is the president. Does that answer your question?" Dunning and the rest of the reporters laughed. "Now, will someone get me a car, or do I have to walk?"

As she exited the hotel, a beggar came up with his hand out. "Can you spare a dime, miss? I need to eat."

"Get that bum outta here," one of the honor guard shouted.

Before the beggar could be pushed aside, Alice took his arm. "Let me talk to him," she said, taking him aside.

While the photographers and reporters had a field day, Alice opened her purse and took out a five-dollar bill. "Here. Will this buy you enough food to get by on?"

The toothless beggar was suddenly aware of the tattered and filthy rags he was wearing. "It's more than enough."

"Where do you live? Do you have a home?" Alice asked.

The beggar pushed back his long, scraggly hair and looked into her eyes. "I got a wife and kids on the poor side of town."

"How many miles away is that?" Alice asked.

"Ain't miles, just a few blocks," he stammered. "Just the other side of daylight over there," he said, pointing down the street.

"Miss Roosevelt . . . er, Mrs. Longworth, it's time to go," said Sgt. Newman.

Alice ignored him and took out another five-dollar bill. "Will you show me where you live?" she asked the beggar.

He looked at the bill, which he needed desperately, but pushed it back. "You don't want to go there. It's too dangerous for a lady."

"But your wife and children live there."

"But they ain't your type," he said.

"They're people aren't they?" she asked.

"Yes, ma'm, but—"

Alice put the five-dollar bill into his pocket. "Then they're my type." She turned to her escorts. "Sgt. Newman, this man, Mr. . . . ." She turned to the beggar. "What's your name?"

"Dennis."

"What's your last name?"

"Alley."

"Sgt. Newman, I have hired this man, Mr. Dennis Alley, to give us a guided tour of St. Louis on the way to the Olympics."

"With all due respect, ma'm," Sgt. Newman said, "he's a bum."

"Let's just say that I'm curious at how the people of St. Louis live."

"But, Mrs. Longworth," said the mayor's aide, "that's the wrong side of town. That's where the—"

Alice cut him off. "I know. That's where the poor people live. But it's the little people who elected my father." She turned to the beggar. "Mr. Alley, please climb into my motor car and show my driver the way."

The mayor's aide stood flabbergasted, watching her drive away.

CHAPTER 21

POOR SIDE OF TOWN

"Now, Mr. Alley, tell the driver where to go," Alice said, sitting in the back seat of the open car.

"Straight ahead, two blocks, then go left." The beggar sat back looking around.

"Anything wrong?" she asked.

"I ain't never ridden in a motor car before," he said, feeling the leather seats. "And I ain't never talked to a president's daughter before."

"So you know who I am?" she smiled, pleased with his recognition.

"Everybody knows who you are Alice . . . er, Miss Roosevelt."

"Just call me Alice."

Her ears caught the strains of German and Irish in the air. The cabbie honked his horn at some friends on a street corner.

"Turn here," the beggar said.

The world turned from day to night in the space of two blocks. From glittering hotels to grimy slums. Though Alice had seen poverty around the world, and had seen pictures of the crowded tenaments of New York, she had never seen anything like this first hand.

"This ain't a pretty sight . . . Alice," the beggar said.

Alice nodded, not knowing what to say. Though she had a reputation as a wild, good-times girl, under the fancy clothes and dresses beat the heart of her father. A person who cared for the underdog and fought the wealthy and entrenched political groups to take care of the underclass.

What she saw was beyond her imagination. *The poor always seem invisible,* she thought, *because wealthy people make it a point never to cross paths with those on the other side of the tracks.*

She thought about her own life, a life of wealth and spoiled privilege. A wave of guilt swept over her.

"Maybe you ought to drop me off here," the beggar said, sensing her mood.

"No, let's continue."

Alice sat quietly, feeling the haunting eyes piercing her from every direction. The specter of disease and death loomed over the foul-smelling streets as rats scurried back and forth.

The ride took them through narrow streets with squeezed-in stores. Houses seemed to touch the gutters. Filthy, dirty bedding hung from windows, and trash cans overflowed with refuse.

Alice felt the depressed sadness in the air. It was such a complete contrast to the opulent wealth just a few blocks away. For the first time in her life, Alice was confused and unsure of herself and her country. *Is this America?* she thought. *Is this what they all came here for? Is this the vision on which my father was elected?*

Pale-faced children scampered down the alleys, kicking cans and fighting over nothing. They were everywhere. Kids, dirty-faced, ill-clothed, and hungry, raced along with the cab.

"Get out of here," the cabbie shouted. "We got no change for you."

Alice opened her purse and pulled out a handful of coins, tossing them to the children. A near riot ensued as the children fought for the coins.

"Don't be doin' that, lady!" the cabbie shouted. "I don't want to get robbed down here."

"I'm sorry, I was just trying to give them some money."

The beggar shrugged. "A little bit don't help the lot of 'em. Just hold tight on your purse."

Alice looked around, contrasting it all with her own upbringing. Beautiful estates with manicured grounds; not foul, dank streets. She and her brothers racing through the fields, barefoot and free; not playing barefoot admist broken glass and piles of disease-filled refuse.

A baby in a diaper long past dirty, sat crying on the steps of a crumbling building. Flies were thick around the lip of his crusted milk cup. "These kids look hungry. That's awful," Alice said.

"Between milkmen mixing water and chalk to stretch the milk and grocers so-called fortifin' sugar with sand, it's a wonder they're even alive," the beggar said.

"Chalk in milk?" Alice asked.

"It's a bad time to be poor in America," he said. "We got the world against us."

Alice shook her head. "That's the worst thing I've ever heard."

"There's worse," the cabbie added, sensing that Alice was someone who could be talked to. "Some of the groceries stretch their dollars by mixin' pieces of dead animals into the butter. Weren't that way when I was growin' up."

Pieces of dead animals mixed in butter? Alice could hardly believe it. Then she noticed them. Dead horses lay on the streets, pulled only far enough out of the road so wagons could get by.

"Why are these horses left on the streets?" she asked the cabbie.

"Just waitin' on the dead animal wagon."

Alice looked down at the bloated animal the children were playing around. "Why are there so many dead horses on these streets?"

The cabbie shrugged. " 'Cause they die of heatstroke, disease, thirst . . . whatever."

Alice shuddered as they rode past. "This is terrible."

On the next corner, boys were pitching pennies when a fight broke out. The cabbie pressed the gas and sped away.

The beggar shook his head. "Bein' poor ain't never pretty. Rich folks, they never look down from their marble mansions to see how bad most really have it."

Alice looked up at the faces peering down from the crowded tenaments around her. "Why doesn't somebody do something about all this?" she asked, holding her nose at the foul smells coming from every direction.

"Do what?" the cabbie laughed. "Your father made a name for himself in New York crusading to help the poor."

"He did help them." She remembered her father's words. *The battle with the slum began the day civilization recognized in it her enemy.*

"Now he's in the fancy White House. You tell him not to forget the little people who elected him."

"You can let me off here, the beggar said. There's my wife."

Alice looked and saw a woman with two small children bundled under her stand, selling four-day-old, stale bread. Alice wanted to help, but she also wanted out of the slum. She didn't want to see or think about any of it.

The cab stopped and the beggar turned to Alice. "Thank you for the ride home."

Alice pulled a few more bills from her purse. "This is for your wife and children. Buy some fresh milk." She pressed the money into his hand.

"I appreciate it, ma'm, but it won't wash away what you seen."

"I wish I could do something about it all," Alice said sincerely.

The beggar shrugged. "One person can't change all of anything. But if you do something to change the life of one person, then you've done something good."

"Good luck," Alice said, taking a deep breath, hoping to forget what she'd seen.

"Thanks," he said, stepping down.

Alice watched him walk away. A sense of emptiness came over her. *I have always closed my eyes to it all, hiding away behind my father. Take away the White House and our money and we have the same needs as these people. We all want to eat, sleep, protect our children, have a roof over our heads. We're all human.*

"You ready to go to the freak show?" the cabbie asked.

She nodded. "I'm ready now," she said, jolted back as the cab took off. *I've never been more ready in my life.*

When the cab turned the corner, the world changed back to what she was used to. The way of wealth, money, and commerce. Signs proclaiming sales and what could be had by those who had money seemed to stretch in all directions.

Fifteen minutes later, the cabbie turned. "Okay, Mrs. Longworth, here's the Olympics."

CHAPTER 22

St. Louis Choo-Choo

The Younguns were dressed in their Sunday clothes sitting like little angels in the back of the wagon. Rev. Youngun turned to his children. "This is how I want you children to act for Mr. Springer the entire time you're with him."

"Yes, Pa," they all said in unison.

Maurice turned and smiled. "You all remember what your Pa just said. You all got to be little angels on this trip or I'll bring you straight home."

Terry rolled his eyes when Maurice turned back around. "I'm hungry," he said, peeking into his *Deadwood Dick* dime novel. It was a story about spotting muggers.

"You just had breakfast," said Sherry.

"Travelin' always makes me hungry," Terry said, moaning.

"You better put that away," Larry said, looking at Terry's book.

Terry gave Larry the evil eye. "Don't rat on me," he said.

"Don't need to rat. You always manage to rat yourself by doin' somethin' stupid."

"And, Terry," Rev. Youngun said over his shoulder, "no tricks at this dog show."

"Dangit don't need no tricks," Larry said, patting the homemade cage they'd made for Dangit from an orange crate from Bedal's General Store.

Terry looked around and when no one was looking, checked the contents of his church coat pocket. *That's good,* he thought. *Got my ventrillo, five stink bombs, two smoke bombs, some sneezin' powder and . . .* he felt the back of his waist band. *Yup, my slingshot is ready to go. No tellin' what else I'll need against those St. Louis muggers.*

Larry looked at Terry and his eyes popped. He slid over and whispered, "Pa said no tricks."

"No tricks at the dog show. He didn't say nothin' 'bout fightin' off muggers."

"There's Old Lady Fury," Sherry said, pointing to the woman in front of her house, howing a garden. "She's mean."

"Don't say that," Rev. Youngun said. "She's just old."

"She's mean and old," Sherry said, pouting.

"Mrs. Fury threw an apple at her last summer, Pa," Larry said, "for no reason at all."

Terry picked up a pebble from the floor of the wagon, pulled out his slingshot and let loose a long shot that hit Mrs. Fury in the behind. She fell forward, grabbing her backside like she'd been stung by a hornet.

Maurice just happened to turn around at that exact moment. He shook his head and mouthed, *Give it to me.*

Terry mouthed, *No.*

Maurice was flustered and mouthed, *Give it to me right now.*

Terry stuck the slingshot back under his coat and mouthed, *I won't do it anymore. Promise.*

Maurice rolled his eyes and mouthed, *I'll bet.*

Sherry, who watched the silent conversation between them, didn't know what to think. "What are you lip talkin' about?"

Larry turned. "I didn't say anything."

"No, Terry," she said, pointing to her brother.

Larry was perplexed. "I didn't hear him say anything either."

Rev. Youngun slowed the wagon. "Here's the train station. And there's your train."

Stopped at the station in a cloud of smoke, the St. Louis Special was waiting to get back on the rails. "We'll miss you, Pa," Sherry said, hugging her father.

"And I'll miss you, little pumpkin." Rev. Youngun looked at the boys. "I mean it. You obey Mr. Springer. He's the boss on this trip."

Maurice smiled on the surface but knew inside the Younguns were their own bosses. *I'm doin' all this for a free trip to the World's Fair,* Maurice thought. *I hope it's all worth it.*

The Younguns waved good-bye to their father. Each carried a bag and fell into line behind Maurice, who carried Dangit in the homemade crate. The station was packed with people going to the Fair and the conductor shouted out, "Standing room only. Sorry folks."

The crowd groaned and Maurice shook his head. "Hope you got your standin' feet on, cause it's a long way to St. Louis."

"We'll find seats," Terry said.

"Don't be too sure of yourself," Larry said.

Terry grinned. "Wanna bet?"

Maurice tapped them both and pointed to the step. "Come on, step up here. Train's 'bout to leave."

They followed behind Maurice, lost in a sea of legs and suitcases all around them. Larry kept his eyes on Sherry and his worries on Terry. They got to the middle of the car and couldn't move any further. As the train started to move, everyone began to push and shove.

"Mr. Springer," Sherry cried, "someone stepped on my foot."

Maurice put Dangit in the overhead rack, then reached down and picked her up. "Can't hold you the whole way, but I'll do my best."

Terry, who didn't want to stand, looked around. There wasn't a seat anywhere, not even in the overhead baggage rack. He looked at the gruff-looking man hogging the seat next to where he was standing and tapped him. He had placed his bags beside him so nobody else except his wife could sit down.

"Can you squeeze over a bit so I can sit down?"

The man shook his head. "It's my seat and my wife and I got here first."

"But I don't feel good. I need to sit down," Terry said.

The man shrugged. "Bathroom's in the back."

Terry wasn't pleased and thought about it all. *I tried being polite and asked nicely. Adults are supposed to help kids, especially sick kids.*

Terry gave the man and his wife the once-over and decided that something was wrong with them. *Maybe they are muggers or bank robbers,* Terry thought. He pulled out his *Deadwood Dick* dime novel and scanned the pages, then looked again at the couple. *They look like bandits,* he decided.

Terry had brought along his arsenal to fight off muggers and worked himself into a frenzy thinking that these were candy thieves. They were out to steal the candy in his bag he wasn't supposed to bring along. It was also his sworn duty, as a paid-for, badge-carrying member of the Deadwood Dick Kid Posse, to fight crime before it started.

Terry looked around, then moved forward with his plan. He made sure no one was looking, then slipped one of the small, glass stink bomb vials from his pocket and bent down as if tying his shoe. He put the nose bomb under his heel and stood back up. When he was sure no one was looking, he stepped down hard.

Crack! Though only Terry heard it in all the commotion, he was sure that everyone on the train would be grabbing him for the police. But no one noticed, so Terry moved away as the terrible rotten-egg stench seeped up from the floor.

Sherry sniffed. Larry held his nose, and Maurice made a terrible expression.

The man who was hogging the seat held his nose.

"Oh, gosh," his wife said, "this is awful. I can't sit here any longer. Come on," she said, standing up, "let's move to another car."

Still holding his nose, her husband said, "All the cars are filled up."

"Well take me to the dining car. I'm hungry," she said, pulling him along.

Before the seats were cold, Terry slid in and pulled Larry and Sherry along with him. He patted the space on the end. "Sit down, Mr. Springer."

Maurice looked down and saw the broken vial on the floor. He eyeballed Terry and said, "Did you do somethin'?"

Terry shook his head. "Not me, my tummy feels all right."

"I ain't talkin' 'bout your tummy. I'm talkin' 'bout this here broken glass on the floor."

Sherry and Larry both looked down then turned and looked at Terry, who just shrugged. "Thought they were muggers. Sorry."

Maurice shook his head and grinned. "Don't go fightin' any more muggers without askin' me first."

Maurice scrunched down into his seat and put his head back, closing his eyes. "Now, maybe you just dropped it and maybe you just happened to step on it and then those two didn't like the smell, they moved, and we got the seats. Yeah, that sounds 'bout right."

Within thirty seconds, Maurice was snoring away. Sherry

got sleepy watching him sleep. She leaned her head against his arm and took a nap.

Larry shook his head. "You were lucky that time. You better watch out."

"We got to sit down, didn't we?"

"Yeah," Larry nodded, "but those things really stink."

CHAPTER 23

THROUGH TAO'S EYES

Mr. Tao stood in the pygmy hut that had been built as a tourist attraction in the Olympic village. He knew that many of the people recruited for the events would never make it back to their homelands, and most of them would never survive in America.

He had come to talk further with Bambuti, the African pygmy who had attracted so much media attention. Though the newspapers and Olympic promoters thought he was a primitive person, Tao had managed to find out his secrets.

There was something about Tao's eyes—his four pupils—that mesmerized people. He had urged Bambuti to come work with him, to live with his traveling crew of different people and make a new life for himself. But Bambuti wanted to go home. The only problem was money—he didn't have enough to get home.

He had pledged to keep Bambuti's knowledge of English a secret. Tao looked around. Not seeing any guards or tourists, he said, "This woman, this reporter is different. I think you should talk with her." Bambuti shook his head. "But a story about you could help raise money to get you home."

Bambuti shook his head again and closed his eyes. He wanted to be home again, home in Africa, back with the little people.

There was a commotion outside and Tao looked through the hut's window. "It is Alice Roosevelt," Tao said, shaking his head. Bambuti turned to his friend, not understanding. Tao shrugged. "She is the daughter of the president of this country, a man like your king." Bambuti nodded.

A dozen reporters followed Alice through the Olympic village. The mayor's aide, who had waited frantically at the gate for Alice to arrive, determined not to lose sight of her again.

Alice was not in the mood for his tour, and her irritation clearly showed. All she could think about were the slums and tenements she'd seen.

The mayor's aide stopped her at the mock Japanese village. "What do you think of Japan's midgets?"

The media entourage following waited for her answer. But she didn't respond.

"Seriously, don't you just love these little Japanese people?"

The small Japanese lined up in front of her and bowed, then shouted *"Banzai! Banzai!"*

She smiled and bowed back. To the media, she said, "When I went to Japan last year, they said a million Japanese had lined the streets of Tokyo, shouting that same word. I think it means hello or something. But I really wish it meant, 'you're the prettiest girl in the world.' "

Flashes popped and everyone within hearing range smiled.

Jack Dunning, from *The St. Louis Post-Dispatch*, called out, "Miss Roosevelt, I . . ."

Alice smiled, trying to loosen up for her father's sake. "Remember, I'm married now."

"Sorry. Mrs. Longworth, how does St. Louis society compare to that of Washington and New York?"

"It's come a long way," she said with a wink, "but there's always room for improvement."

"What do you think of all these barbarians gathered together?" shouted a reporter.

"I think it's kind of exciting to see all these people of different shapes and sizes in one place," she answered. But to Dunning she whispered, "This is something right out of the *Tales of Sinbad*."

Dunning pointed to Bambuti, who stood outside his hut watching all the commotion. "They call that one a pygmy. He's straight from Africa."

"Hey, Alice," a reporter shouted. "How 'bout a picture of you and the pygmy standing side by side."

Alice waved to Bambuti, but he didn't respond. "Can . . . I . . . have . . . picture . . . taken . . . with . . . you," she said, as if talking to a child. Bambuti did nothing but stare into her eyes. "Does someone know how to talk to him?" Alice asked, looking around. "I'd like my picture taken with this one."

Tao stood just inside the hut, shaking his head. It was time to meet the Wilders, so he slipped out the other door, leaving Bambuti and the president's daughter in a blaze of camera flashes.

At the edge of the Olympic grounds, Laura and Manly got out of a cab in a dusty field. Manly looked around and questioned the cabbie.

"Why you lettin' us off here?" Manly asked.

The cabbie shrugged. "The road's too bad up there. I don't want to get stuck in a ditch."

"Where's the Olympics? I don't see a stadium."

"Ain't none. That's Washington University over there, where most everything's bein' held. Walk on over, but watch out for panhandlers."

Manly shrugged and took Laura's hand. They stepped carefully through the field, trying to avoid the mudholes and cowpies. Laura saw a policeman sitting on a box next to the track-and-field entrance fence and decided to ask him for directions.

"Can you tell me where we could find the Anthropology Day events?"

The policeman pointed behind him. "In there." He said something else, but a roar from the crowd blocked his answer.

"I didn't hear," Laura said.

"I said, if you hurry on in and get a seat in the bleachers, you'll still have a chance to see 'em."

"See who?"

The policeman looked at Laura as if she was crazy. "See the freaks! They're havin' a march of the misfits right 'bout now. It's the most popular event of the Olympics so far."

The crowd roared again. Manly took Laura's arm. "Come on, honey, let's go see for ourselves."

"But Mr. Tao said to meet him here."

"Well, where is he?" Manly asked, irritated by the heat and dust.

"I am here," Tao said, standing behind them.

"Oh, Mr. Tao, we were worried that you'd forgotten," Laura said.

"No, I was worried you wouldn't come. Please come, the events are starting."

Once inside the gate, they were surrounded by drunks. Lines to the beer stands snaked under the stands. Foul, vulgar language was tossed about all around them.

A big, burly man tripped against Manly and snapped, "Get the—" He stopped in mid-sentence, looking at Mr. Tao's eyes.

"You should watch your language," Mr. Tao said coldly to the man.

The intoxicated man tipped his hat to Laura. "Sorry, lady, didn't know you were here."

Manly pulled Laura along, whispering, "Why don't we leave now. I don't care 'bout seein' no freaks."

Mr. Tao smiled. "Seems like there are freaks all around us." he bowed, then looked around at the drunks.

"This whole thing sounds like a bad joke," Laura said.

"Some jokes depend on who is doing the telling and who the jokes are about," Tao said, walking toward the stairs.

Once up in the stands, Laura saw it wasn't a joke. It was a tragedy. The announcer called out, "And here's what you've all been waiting for: the parade of the most unusual people the world has ever seen gathered together. We call it the parade of misfits!"

The drunken crowd cheered and jeered as a long line of humans of all shapes and sizes walked out onto the field. More than two thousand people of different colors and sizes were paraded in front of the crowd. Dressed in their native costumes, they were encouraged to dance around.

More than seventy-five thousand people crowded into the stands and around the field, watching the parade.

Tao tapped Laura and whispered, "I have always wondered how people can get such great pleasure laughing about others." Laura didn't respond.

On the reviewing platform, Alice watched the parade of athletes walk by.

"Oh, Mrs. Longworth, look at the Indians," said the mayor's aide. "And that's Chief Geronimo himself," he said, pointing to the legendary Indian chief, leading the procession of American Indians.

The announcer called out the names of the Indian leaders and the thirteen different tribes on the field. "And this is

White Horse, Chief of the Iowas; this is Jalahai, Chief of the Sioux."

Running behind the chief of the Sioux came the Pawnee, Sioux, Crow, Black White Bears, and a stately group of Navaho. "And challenging our own Indians are tribes like these," the announcer screamed, pointing out the Kafirs, Maricabos, Syrians, the Batatela tribe from the Congo, and a dancing group of Africans, brandishing spears.

"This is truly a meeting of barbarians!" the announcer shouted to the applause of the crowd.

Laura watched in silence, disgusted with the degrading performance of the people around her. She turned to Manly. "This is outrageous."

Manly sighed. "If they came of their own free will, ain't much you can do about it."

Mr. Tao slowly shook his head. "They were tricked into coming here, thinking it was a sporting event."

The crowd kept laughing as tall, small, or deformed American Indians were paraded along with Patagonians, a miniature Cuban, and Bambuti. Mr. Tao closed his eyes when he saw the hurt in his little friend's eyes.

"Look at that miniature spear-chucker," laughed the man in front of Laura. "He ain't no more'n three feet tall!"

Laura saw Tao staring intently at the field, and followed his eyes to the pygmy. She looked at the pygmy, and for a moment their eyes locked. His intense loneliness and humiliation showed in that brief second which passed as his eyes scanned the crowd. Then he began to dance and sing in circles for the audience.

Alice watched with dismay. "Is it almost over?"

The mayor's aide smiled. "Over? It's just begun. These

strange people are going to compete in events so we can compare them to the civilized people of the world."

The crowd cheered when some of the Indians did backflips and the announcer continued. "Some of the events will be spectacular, some will be lively, and all will be fun to watch. No where else has there ever been gathered Africans, giant Patagonians, all the tribes of American Indians we could find, Filipinos, Eskimos, Cliff-Dwellers, Kafirs, Hinus, Singhalese, and an African pygmy. Over two thousand of these strange things have been brought here for your enjoyment."

Brandishing their spears, shields, and bows and arrows, the Africans danced forward, pretending they were hunting the crowd. The announcer laughed, "We're gonna have all these strange people showin' you how they live in their jungles and forests. We'll even have a mixed group of them over in a pen at the end of the track for you to look at."

"A human zoo," Tao whispered.

"What did you say?" Laura asked.

"It sounds like a human zoo." He turned to look at Laura. "Have you ever been to the zoo and seen the unhappy animals all penned together?" Laura nodded. "Well, come with me, I want you to see how the world looks through my eyes."

Two men dressed in Safari clothes came from inside the tent and pushed the athletes along toward their mock villages. "What some people will do for publicity," Alice said quietly.

"Do you want to walk back through the villages?" the mayor's aide asked. "You can even touch them if you like."

Alice glared. "These are human beings you're talking about. Not barn animals." She stood up. "Mr. Dunning, will you take me back to the Ritz?"

"It would be a pleasure," he said, taking her arm and walking off into a barrage of camera flashes.

Laura walked silently through the mock villages between Tao and Manly.

"This is humanity gone mad," Tao said quietly. "It is the worst of humanity taking control."

"Hard to tell who the keepers are, or should be," Manly said, watching two drunks harass Chief Geronimo.

They walked toward the pen but had a hard time getting close enough to see much. There were so many people crowding around, staring and laughing at the strange people assembled from around the world, Manly had to push their way to the front.

"What kind of events will they have for these men?" Manly asked Tao.

"Whatever will bring a laugh," Tao said.

A club-footed Indian limped the perimeter of the pen and stopped to stare at Manly. After he walked away, Tao said, "He will be a contestant in the mud fight."

"Mud fight? What kind of Olympic contest is that?" Laura asked.

"This is not a contest. This is just a way for people to laugh at other people and for the promoters to make money. Greed brings out the worst in all people."

Laura drifted away to look closer at the men in the pen. She stared at the unhappy group, some begging for food. Then she saw him. The small, dark African pygmy was on his knees at the far side of the pen, as far away from the crowd as he could get.

He almost looks as if he's praying, Laura thought, as she watched his mouth move silently above his clasped hands. The little man touched his forehead, than turned and locked eyes with Laura for the second time.

One of the men who had moved the anthropology athletes into the pen was also watching the pygmy. Laura walked over to him and asked, "Do any of these people speak English? I'm a reporter and I'd like to talk with one of them."

The man shrugged. "I don't think any of them are smart enough."

The pygmy seemed to be listening to them. It was difficult for Laura to look at him, and she turned away. But she had seen something, and slowly turned back to look into the eyes of the little man.

There was a single tear, working its way down the dark cracks and crevices of his face. Laura walked over and knelt down beside him, looking at him as if she were trying to communicate with someone from outer space.

"Hello," she whispered. "I wish I knew why you were so sad. I wish you knew how to speak so I could know what you are thinking."

The pygmy blinked, then lowered his head, sobbing silently. Laura wanted to reach across the pen and comfort him, but the rail seemed like the biggest barrier in the world. "What is your name?" she asked softly, not expecting an answer.

The pygmy looked up from his hands and said, "Bambuti."

Laura was startled. "Your name is Bambuti? Oh how I wish you spoke English. There are so many things I want to ask you. Like why you're crying right now."

Bambuti looked into Laura's eyes and said in a halting, clipped British accent, "I am crying because I am all alone at the edge of the world."

"You speak English?" Laura whispered, looking around as if she were doing something wrong.

The men in the safari suits stepped into the pen. "Okay, back to your cages."

"What are you doing here? How did you get here? Where are you—"

Laura was cut off by a big man pushing Bambuti along. Before Laura could stop him, the pygmy reached over and squeezed Laura's hand. "I am so sad because the center of the forest seems so far away."

"Move it!" shouted a policeman, prodding Bambuti forward with his baton. He kicked Bambuti to the ground, and before Laura could say anything, Bambuti whispered. "Don't tell anyone, I want to win my freedom." He looked terribly sad. "I am not an animal. I am a man."

Laura watched the little man walk away, their eyes locked until he was out of sight. Manly came up and put his arm around her. "Not a pretty sight, is it, girl?"

"He talked, Manly. He talked."

"That's what I've been trying to tell you, Mrs. Wilder," Tao said. "They are all human beings."

"I wish I knew more about him," Laura said, still stunned.

Mr. Tao took her hands in his. "What would you like to know?"

"You know him?"

Mr. Tao nodded. "Come, let us find a place to talk. Then I'll introduce you to Bambuti."

As they walked away, Laura clutched Manly's sleeve. "Oh, Manly, he talked to me. He said, 'I am a man.' "

CHAPTER 24

BAMBUTI'S STORY

hey found a shady spot, and Mr. Tao said, "To understand Bambuti, you have to understand how long the world has been fascinated by pygmys. From the dawn of time, exotic tales about pygmies are part of every culture."

"The word *pygmy* is Greek and was derived from a unit of measure, the distance between a man's knuckles and his elbow."

"I hope you're leading up to telling us about Bambuti," Manly said. "'Cause I used to fall asleep in school."

Mr. Tao bowed slightly. "I enjoy knowledge," he said, "but I will save what I know for another time."

"For Bambuti, the idyllic life of his first five years, living in the forests in central Africa with his family, hunting with his father, being taught about the god of all forests by his grandfather, was everything life should be. His mother doted over him and taught him the songs and dances of the people. But life soon became difficult."

"What happened?" Laura asked.

"When he was five years old, Sir Henry Morton Stanley, the famous African explorer, reached the Ituri forest in 1887 and captured four women, several men, and a boy. Bambuti was the boy, one of the men his father, and one of the women his mother."

"Captured," Laura said, "that sounds horrible."

"It was how the slaves were brought to this country. Bambuti was captured to work for Stanley, but that wasn't much better. Stanley wrote all about it in his book *In Darkest Africa.*"

"I haven't read it," Laura said.

"You should," Mr. Tao chided. "In my eyes, it stands as a testament to man's inhumanity to man." He bowed slightly. "I am sorry. I'm digressing."

"Please, I want to hear what you have to say," Laura said.

"Stanley took Bambuti and his parents along on his journey across Africa, fighting through hostile Ituri forests against the non-pygmy tribes who used poison arrows.

"In one of the battles, Bambuti's father was severely wounded and was left behind. Bambuti told me he would never forget the arrow sticking out from his father's side as his mother pulled him away."

"How sad," Laura said, shaking her head.

"Most of the others were killed before Stanley reached Ujiji. His mother was sold in the Arab slave market there for eighty yards of sheeting cloth."

"Stanley sold Bambuti's momma?" Manly asked, astounded.

Tao nodded. "Bambuti told me that he remembers wailing, trying to hold on to his mother's legs as she was dragged away by the trader who bought her." Tao paused, remembering the emotional moment when Bambuti had told him this.

"The poor boy," Laura said.

Tao nodded. "Evidently, he impressed an elderly white missionary couple from England, the Chandlers. They bought Bambuti for the price of sixteen yards of sheeting cloth, gave him freedom, and unofficially adopted him.

"They spoke a smattering of his language and as they traveled across Africa, they taught him to speak English. Though he missed his parents, the Chandlers treated him well—and kept him from the slavers."

"So it had a happy ending," Manly said.

"It was happy for a while. For the next five years he called them Mum and Poppa. But the Chandlers were killed by a group of black slavers on the journey to Capetown."

"What happened then?" Manly asked, hanging on to Tao's every word.

"Bambuti kept the secret that he understood English from the slavers, because they killed those who spoke English. He was kept tied to a walking pole as the slavers stole women and children to take to the slave markets in Zanzibar."

"And then?" Manly whispered.

"Let Mr. Tao speak," Laura said, chiding her husband.

Tao bowed in thanks. "In Zanzibar, he managed to escape through a small hole in the thatched ceiling and fled on foot down the coast. When he reached Zambezi, he obtained work entertaining British soldiers with the dances he remembered doing as a boy."

"Why'd he come to these games?" Manly asked.

"A British officer, familiar with the Anthropology Days contest, saw Bambuti dancing for coins. He had his helper, who knew a smattering of the Ituri forest people's language, tell Bambuti that if he won, he could have fifty pounds sterling as his prize."

"But he speaks English! Why didn't he tell the officer?" Manly asked.

Tao shrugged. "He continued to keep the secret of knowing English to himself. He found his tips were bigger by listening to the British soldiers and dancing and singing the forest songs just as they wanted, without their knowing he was eavesdropping on them."

"He wants to win the money to get home," Laura nodded.

"Fifty pounds is more money than Bambuti has ever seen," Tao said. "It's enough to buy passage back to his forest home. Back to the free place of his dreams."

"What can be done to help him?" Laura asked.

"I have offered him work, to come join my family of different people, but he is convinced that the only way home lies in winning the contest."

"This sounds like something out of a book," Laura said.

"It could be," Tao agreed. "Bambuti was kept in the dank bottom of an old steamship for four weeks, until he arrived in New York and rode by train to St. Louis. It was as if he had left the earth and entered a terrifying place where everyone made fun of him."

"Most folks would have given up tryin' to get home a long time ago," Manly said.

"He is sustained by the dream of seeing the center of the forest again, the place his grandfather showed him," Tao said.

"Is there such a place?" Manly questioned.

Tao nodded. "He believes there is. The memory has kept him alive all these years."

"I want to meet him," Laura said.

CHAPTER 25

PYGMY'S PRAYER

ambuti reached into the bucket that was passed to him. He sniffed the rancid piece of buffalo meat and wished for the fruits and vegetables of the forest.

A giant man grunted and indicated that Bambuti should eat. Bambuti shook his head and handed back the food. The giant shrugged as if the pygmy was crazy, but happily ate his portion of the dinner.

Bambuti went to the corner, seeking a space where he could be alone, and got down on his knees. He put his hands over his eyes.

Please let me go to where my grandfather took me. Please let me win the contests so that I can return to the forests and be with my people.

Mr. Tao lead Laura and Manly to Bambuti's hut. The guard looked at Tao's eyes and looked down. "What do you want?"

"Mrs. Wilder is a newspaper reporter. She would like to talk to . . . him," Tao said, pointing to Bambuti.

"He can't understand a word you say."

"She knows sign language," Mr. Tao said, smiling.

The guard signaled to Bambuti with a nudge of his stick

and said, "I know you understand this." He poked him again. "This newspaper lady wants to write 'bout you." Tao nodded to Bambuti and made a sign with his fingers. Bambuti brightened when he saw Laura, the lady who had first spoken to him with her eyes.

The guard took them to another hut, then left. Tao said, "Bambuti, this is the woman I told you about."

Laura knelt down. "Bambuti, I know you don't want to speak, but no one is listening. Please tell me about you. I really want to know."

Bambuti looked at her and believed in her sincerity. He nodded. "What would you like to know?" he asked.

"Mr. Tao has told me about Stanley taking you from your forest and about how you got here." Bambuti looked down for a moment, remembering it all, then looked back up into her eyes. "He said you had been to the center of the forest. Would you tell me about it, please?"

Tao nodded. "She is sincere."

"You want to know about the center of the forest?" Bambuti asked.

"Yes. Please tell me." Laura answered.

"Tell it from your dream thoughts," Tao said quietly. Laura looked at Tao with a questioning look in her eyes. Tao said to her, "That is his way. It is the way he has taught himself to escape from the world that mistreats him."

Bambuti thought as hard as he could and felt the peaceful dreaming come on again. The memories came back to him as he drifted off, narrating his dream from the memories long kept locked in his mind.

With his eyes closed, he said, "Where I come from, everyone is small like me. Most people are light brown, reddish in color. Some of them are yellowish. All the colors of the forest that I remember."

Laura started to speak, but Mr. Tao held up his finger for silence.

"Smiles. Smiles everywhere. No tall people. No one larger than four tall man's feet on top of each other. The men of my people have marks on their arms and stomachs. The pretty women, naked and smiling, tend to children and clean their small huts.

"Children play amidst the leaf piles, picking at the monkey cooking on the fire spit. My father stretches an animal skin, and my mother pulls bananas from the bunches stacked alongside the fire pit.

"Food wrapped in leaves is on the hot coals, and old people look out from their beehive-shaped huts, smelling the high-sun meal of the day." He opened his eyes suddenly, startling Laura. He smiled, then closed them again.

"Grandfather comes over and takes my hand. 'Bambuti, it is time we went monkey hunting. And time I took you to the special place, to the center of the forest.' I follow Grandfather into the deep woods, as he stalks a troop of swinging monkeys. 'Those are the red colobuses, a good meat,' he says quietly.

" 'Do we eat all monkeys, Grandfather?' I ask, with the curiosity of a young boy. But Grandfather says, 'No, never attack or kidnap a baby gorilla, for the mother will stalk you. She will track you until she has killed you. That is the way of the forest.' "

Bambuti paused, then made the sounds of animals and the cries of birds in his throat. "We are people of the dark woods. The trees block the light. Grandfather has me make the sounds to protect us when we come upon a patch of open space, where two trees had fallen after the earth had pushed up.

" 'Make the sounds again, Bambuti,' Grandfather says. But

a large shadow crosses the ground, and Grandfather covers me over.

" 'What was that?' I ask.

"My grandfather holds out his arms, imitating wings. 'That was the giant eagle. I have only seen him once since I was your age. He is ten feet across and will eat you if he catches you. That is why you should never leave our forests. They can't get you here in the safety of the big leaves.'

"I look up as the shadow crosses again. Grandfather says, 'Remember that sight.'

"He pulls me along, pointing to the largest monkey in a troop of them chattering away. 'That one will lead us into the center of the world if we follow him long enough.'

"I look at the larger-than-the-others monkey. He swings his fist back at us, as if saying to 'go back, don't come any closer.' But Grandfather presses on and grows silent as the forest darkens.

" 'Is the center of the forest cold and dark?' I ask.

" 'No, Bambuti, it is warm and beautiful and filled with butterflies.'

"We get deeper into the forest, to the place that is only spoken about by the old ones around the night fires.

"I remember looking around as if seeing the forest through different eyes, as if the leaves had all changed colors in my mind.

"Then he parts the leaves and points ahead to where the light shows through. 'There is the center of the forest.'

" 'Can we go inside?' I ask my grandfather.

" 'It is not the time. You will know when that is.' "

Bambuti paused, then said quietly, "It is something I will never forget. It was the most beautiful place in the world, the center of the forest of life."

Laura looked at the man her countrymen called a primitive savage. She listened to him express eloquent thoughts and sentiments. "What did the center of the forest look like?" Laura asked.

"Time to go, pygmy," shouted the guard. "There's tourists to entertain."

Bambuti blinked open his eyes, as if coming back from a place far, far away, but he didn't turn his head or show any sign that he understood what the guard had said.

"Can't he stay longer?" Laura asked.

The guard laughed. "God knows you folks are just wastin' your time tryin' to communicate with him. He don't understand nothin' I say. Do you?" he said to Bambuti.

Bambuti stared straight ahead. He was silent.

CHAPTER 26

ALL BOOKED UP

"Wake up. Wake up, Terry," Maurice said, shaking him gently.

Terry had been dreaming of fighting off muggers. He put up his fists and said sleepily, "Outta my way. Don't touch me!"

Larry laughed. "He's dreamin' of bein' a tough guy again."

Terry looked around and blinked, remembering he was on the train to St. Louis. "Are we there?"

Maurice smiled. "Yes sir. Train's about to pull into the station." From above them they heard a loud moaning. Maurice looked up at Dangit. "What's wrong with you, dog?"

Sherry shook her head. "I think he's got to go."

Maurice slapped his forehead. "No, Dangit, not here. That crate's got holes in it."

Terry remembered he was directly underneath and jumped up. "Dangit, no boy. We'll be off in a minute!"

Dangit kept whimpering, so when the train stopped, Maurice carefully picked up the crate, checked for leaks, and quickly pushed his way off the train. The Younguns followed closely behind and managed to get Dangit to a fancy display garden in the middle of the terminal to do his business.

A policeman walked over and eyed the event. "What do you think you're doin'?"

Terry shrugged with his hands and shoulders. "Just fertilizin' the pretty plants." Dangit finished and scurried back into the crate.

The policeman looked at the three kids standing there and shook his head. "Don't be doin' any more fertilizin' in the train station. Those flowers are a gift from the Queen of England."

Maurice knew it was time to go and pushed the kids forward. "Thank you, officer, we won't let that dog do nothin' else around here." He led the children away, right past the newspaper stand. None of them saw the front page of *The St. Louis Post-Dispatch* with their picture on it plastered all over the wall. The blaring headline read:

TALKING DOG WINS MANSFIELD CONTEST!
Down on the farm, they'll believe anything!

By Bret Malcom

As part of my Missouri country living series, I happened to be in Mansfield when they held their local dog show. Expecting to see a bunch of mangy barnyard mutts, I was shocked to see that even in the country, people make fools of themselves over their pets.

What was different about this show, however, was that three slick kids convinced everyone that their dog, Dangit, could talk. They won the contest and the free trip to St. Louis. Now, I know some people will do anything to get off the farm, but you've got to hand it to the three Youngun kids—and their father is a Methodist minister no less—for having the big-city ingenuity to pull such a fast one.

I wish everyone could have seen the local yokels making fools of themselves over the "talking dog," which the kids had somehow managed to make part of a fancy ventriloquist act. If Dangit was running for governor of Missouri, he'd probably win. Which just goes to show that in the "show me state," if you show them a talking dog and they believe it . . . why, they'll believe just about anything.

Who knows? Maybe someone will show us a governor and state legislature who will do something more than just line their pockets! Maybe we should run a "Dangit for Governor" campaign. This way, when he wanted to go for a walk, at least he'd be telling the truth.

The newspaper vendor looked at the picture and then at the kids. "Does that dog really talk?" he shouted out to Maurice.

Maurice didn't hear him, but Terry answered. "Sometimes he does, but he's got laryngitis now." The man laughed.

The Younguns had never before seen so many people—so many different kinds of people—in one place. Terry was a bit worried and constantly needed to pat the outside of his pocket to make sure that he still had his antimugger arsenal.

Outside the station, Maurice lined them up on the curb. "Now, we're goin' to be takin' a cab to the West Side Hotel. There are lots of bad people in big towns like this, so no funny business, you hear?"

"Yea, Mr. Springer," they all said in unison.

While waiting for the cab, Terry saw the organ grinder and his monkey, working the crowd for money again. Every time the monkey put his paw out, someone put a coin in it. The monkey would sniff it, bite it, and put it in the cup on the side of the music box.

Terry was fascinated and drifted off to watch, without Maurice noticing he was gone. When the monkey approached Terry, he stuck out his paw. Terry gave him a nickle, and the monkey shook his hand.

"Pleased to meet you," Terry said, and the crowd around him laughed.

Terry then pulled out a gumdrop and handed it to the monkey. "Don't be a feedin' him candy," the vendor shouted, but it was too late. The monkey ate the gumdrop, jumped around, and kissed Terry on the lips.

"Ah, gosh," Terry said, wiping his lips. "Don't do that again."

The organ grinder tried to get the monkey to come back, but he wanted more candy. Terry gave him another gumdrop, and when he refused to give him another, the monkey climbed onto Terry's back.

"Get him off me!" Terry screamed. The monkey reached into his pockets, took two more gum drops, then pulled out a packet of sneezing powder.

"Don't take that!" Terry shouted, trying to grab it back. But the monkey ripped it open. "Ah-choo, ah-choo," Terry sneezed, over and over as the powder drifted up his own nose.

The monkey sniffed the packet and began sneezing. He dropped the gumdrops and did sneezing back flips, front flips, side rolls, sumersaults, handstands, and cartwheels. When he dropped the packet, the organ grinder picked it up, and he began sneezing.

The monkey, sneezing and chattering, ran into Terry, who tried to put the packet of sneezing powder back in his pocket. The monkey grabbed it and flung it into the air. It broke open in mid-air and the powder spread among the crowd of onlookers.

Suddenly, thirty people were sneezing and bumping into each other. Terry held his nose and brushed past the same policeman who had lectured them inside. The policeman started to ask what was going on but began to sneeze uncontrollably!

Larry was already in the cab and Maurice was lifting Sherry

up as Terry came running over. "Why you holdin' your nose?" Maurice asked, then turned to see the sneezing crowd.

He looked at Terry. "I better not ask. Come on, let's get outta here." He lifted Terry up and climbed in. "Please take us to the West Side Hotel."

The cabbie turned. "Got any money?"

"What kind of question is that?" Maurice asked indignantly, showing him a dollar bill.

"Just askin'. Can't be too sure these days with all the riff-raff comin' to the Fair."

The Younguns gawked like country bumpkins at all the sights and sounds around them. Maurice answered so many "what's that?" questions, that he finally asked for silence.

At the hotel, Maurice paid the fare and gave the cabbie a ten-cent tip, which the cabbie used to buy a paper from a newsboy. He looked at the picture, then turned toward the kids with Maurice as they walked away. He said to another cabbie parked beside him, "I just drove a talking dog."

The other cabbie turned and nodded in sympathy. "I've had a lot of bad fares myself today," he said, and drove off.

Maurice took the Younguns to the front desk and looked at the red-nosed man behind the desk. "You got a room for the Younguns and Maurice Springer?"

The desk clerk eyeballed the black man and three white children standing in front of him. "Who are you?"

"My name is Maurice Springer and these are the Youngun children. We're from Mansfield."

"Ah," he said, holding up the front page, "the talking dog con artists."

The kids looked at each other. "What you talkin' about?" Larry asked.

"This," the desk clerk said, showing him the picture. Larry took the newspaper from his hands and scanned the article.

"What's it say?" Terry asked.

"It says that we got caught. Oh, man," Larry moaned, "what are we goin' to do now?"

"Let's go up to our room and hide under the bed," Sherry suggested.

Maurice looked at the newspaper and closed his eyes. This was another fine mess the Younguns had gotten him into. "May we have our room key, please?"

The desk clerk cut him off. "We're overbooked. Can't help you with a room."

Maurice noticed the "no coloreds" sign on the wall and shook his head. "We got a reservation here," he said, pulling out the letter that Mrs. Bentley had provided them. "Look at it."

The desk clerk took the letter and quickly read it. "Says you had a room all right, but we're overbooked. There must be twenty thousand people in this town for the Fair. Every room in this part of town is booked solid."

"But what about our reservation?" Larry asked.

"Sorry, kid, nothin' I can do about it."

Larry raised his hand. "But we got Dangit, the winner of the dog show with us."

The desk clerk said, "No dogs allowed in here anyway, not even talking dogs."

Dangit began growling from inside the crate.

"Then where are these kids goin' to stay?" Maurice asked. "Can you get us a room elsewhere?"

The desk clerk shook his head. "We're all booked up. Everyone's booked up. And even if there were rooms, I don't know who would let in a black man, three white kids, and a dog. Maybe the YMCA down the street, but I don't think so."

Maurice was humiliated and angry. He turned to the children and asked them to put their hands over their ears. Being kids, they put them on just enough so they could still hear every word.

Maurice looked at the man and signaled with his finger for him to lean closer. "Now, you listen to me. These kids got a room here and you know it. You may not want me here, but you ain't gonna deny them their paid-for room."

The desk clerk started to pull back, but Maurice reached out and held onto his tie, pointing down toward Dangit. "Now, if you don't find them a room in ten seconds, I'm gonna turn Killer loose on your fat rear end, and you won't be able to sit down for a month."

The desk clerk gulped. "I might be able to find these children a room but . . ."

Maurice nodded. "You get them their rightful room and I'll go over and get me a room in black town. Will that be all right?"

"But who will watch them if you're not here to nanny them?"

Maurice dropped the man's tie. "I ain't no nanny or man-servant. I'm their friend and neighbor. I'm sure you got some old granny type workin' in the kitchen who could sit with 'em until I come back after findin' me a place. Right?"

"Why, maybe, I . . ."

Maurice nodded again. "Good. Then go get one up here, now, before I let Killer loose."

"But the dog can't stay, house rules," the desk clerk pleaded.

"I'll take the dog with me. Now go on and get me a granny."

Maurice turned back toward the Younguns who were all shaking their heads. "No way," Larry said, "you ain't leavin' us here with some kitchen granny."

"We're comin' with you, Mr. Springer," Sherry cried, grabbing on to his leg.

"Kids, kids. It'll only be for a little while 'fore I finds Dangit and me a room. There's no room at this inn for Dangit and me, but they can't deny you stayin' here."

"Ain't right," Terry shouted, trying to climb up the counter. "Ain't right."

Maurice took him in his arms. "Some things are goin' to take a long time to change. But just remember, no one can hold back the future." Larry and Sherry leaned closer to hear. "All hate does is grow more hate. So just learn from this that what's in your heart is the most important thing in the world."

"But it ain't right," Terry said, his eyes welling up.

"Time's are changin', little ones," Maurice said, nodding to each of them in turn.

The desk clerk came back with an older woman in tow. "She's got a moustache!" Larry whispered.

"I ain't stayin' with no witch!" Terry shouted, struggling to free himself from Maurice's arms.

The desk clerk cleared his throat. "This is, ah . . . Miss Beatrice Grey. I'm sure you kids will just love her."

Terry turned to Sherry, who was shaking at the sight of the imposing old woman. "I ain't stayin'. Get me a cab outta here!"

"She looks like the bearded lady in the circus," Sherry said, holding her hands over her eyes.

Maurice put his hand over Terry's mouth. "Ah, Miss Grey, these here three children are Larry, Terry, and Sherry Youngun. Their father's a Methodist minister in Mansfield and they're here for the dog show."

Miss Grey nodded and spoke in a deep, deep voice. "I love good children. Are you good children?" she asked.

The Youngun's eyes all went wide. Maurice tapped each of them on the head and they nodded.

Maurice saw the fear on their faces and knelt down in front of them. "I gotta go now, but I'll be back. I promise."

"But we want to be with you!" Sherry said, whimpering.

"I know, I know. I'm gonna go see my cousin Speedy Springer. He runs some kind of rooming house over on the east side. He'll put me and Dangit up."

"Can't Speedy put us up too?" Larry asked.

Maurice shrugged. "I ain't seen Speedy for years. Let me go check things out, then I'll come back over here and get you if things work out. Okay?"

"Okay," they all said in unison.

"Good," said Maurice, standing back up. "Now, Miss Grey, if you'd be so kind as to watch out for these wonderful kids in room . . ." He turned to the clerk, "What room they got?"

"Room 210."

"Okay, if you'd watch these three Younguns in room 210, then I'll go get me a place to stay and be back 'fore supper, all right?"

"That'll be just fine," she said, in the deepest voice the Younguns had ever heard come from a woman.

"That's good," said Maurice. "Now you children be good for Miss Grey, and I'll take Dangit over to Speedy's and be back in a flash."

All three Younguns clung to Maurice as he turned to leave. Miss Grey stepped in and put her hands on Larry's head. "They'll be fine, don't you worry." She turned to the desk clerk. "Give me the room key and we'll go on up and wait."

Maurice picked up Dangit. He felt terrible leaving the Younguns, but he didn't want to chance taking them with him until he knew what kind of place Speedy was running. Dangit moaned as he was taken from the kids. When Maurice disappeared through the front door, the Younguns felt their whole world was collapsing.

"Come with me, children," Miss Grey said, walking away.

The Younguns followed behind, like they were being led to

a witch's den. "If she tries to kiss me, I'm gonna kick her," Terry whispered.

"Maybe she ain't that bad," Larry said, trying to reassure them.

"Don't like bearded ladies," Sherry cried.

Miss Grey stopped at room 210 and opened the door. She herded the Younguns inside and shut the door behind them.

Inside, she crossed her arms and looked at them sternly. "You do what I say, when I say it. If I say jump, you better jump, or I'll smack the tar outta you!" She screamed, "Do you understand me, you little brats?"

They all gulped and barely nodded.

"Now," she said, pacing the room, "I'm going down to the kitchen to have my dinner brought to the room. I'm gonna charge it to your minister daddy. I want you to get out all the money you got hidden away and hand it to me when I get back up here." She slammed the door behind her.

"We ain't gettin' out alive," Terry moaned.

"I want Mr. Springer back!" Sherry cried, throwing herself on the bed.

Larry walked over and looked through the curtains. Maurice was standing by the cab stand, holding Dangit in the crate. "There's Mr. Springer!" Larry shouted. Terry and Sherry crowded around to see.

"Let's get outta here!" Terry said. He ran to the door and tried to open it. "She locked us in!"

"What are we gonna do?" Sherry cried out.

Larry paced. "Let me think . . . let me think." Then he had an idea. "Take the sheets off the beds, quick!" Terry and Sherry stripped the beds down. Then Larry knotted the sheets together, like he'd read about Detective Dick doing, tied them to the bed post, and threw open the window.

"Mr. Springer wait! Wait Mr. Springer!" Larry shouted, but Maurice didn't hear him with all the street nose.

A black cab driver saw Maurice's raised hand and pulled alongside. "Need a lift, my brother?"

"Can you take me to this address?" Maurice asked, showing him the address he'd written down for Speedy Springer.

The cabbie looked Maurice up and down, "You goin' there dressed like that?" he asked, wondering why a man dressed in farmer clothes would be going to a juke joint.

Larry saw that the cab was starting to leave and shouted, "Wait, Mr. Springer."

Sherry started really crying and Larry turned to Terry. "Come on quick!" He tossed the sheet-rope out the window and turned around. "Terry, you go first."

"Why me?"

"'Cause I got to help Sherry. You climb down and I'll drop our bags to you."

"What if it breaks?" Terry asked, looking down.

"You want to take a chance on the sheet breakin' or waitin' for that mean old lady to come back."

Terry began climbing out the windowsill. "I'd rather fall to my death than wait for that bearded witch to kill me."

He climbed down like a monkey and caught the cloth bags that Larry dropped to him. A car was stalled in front of the cab, so the cabbie was talking with Maurice while they waited for the owner to push his vehicle out of the way. Dangit was in the crate in the back and started to bark when he saw Terry on the ground.

Larry pleaded, "Come on, Sherry, climb down, I'll help you."

Sherry put her hands over her eyes. "I'm scared of tall places."

"You want to stay and play with that lady?"

"No!" she screamed.

Larry started out the window. "Then you better come on. I'll be right in front of you and . . ."

"Let me get on your back, please!" she cried, and before Larry could protest, she was clinging to him tighter than a baby possum.

Larry went down the sheet rope arm-over-arm with Sherry on his back, and they hit the ground running. "Grab a bag, come on!" he shouted to them. "Mr. Springer! Wait, Mr. Springer!" he shouted, running as fast as he could.

But Maurice couldn't hear them with all the traffic noise and the cab pulled slowly away. Terry ran ahead, tossed his bag next to Dangit, and climbed onto the flat bed in the back. Sherry was falling behind, so Larry grabbed her under one arm and lifted her up. The cab started to speed up. Terry reached out his hand to Larry.

"Come on, Larry, you can make it!"

Larry got a second wind. The cabbie turned, "What's goin' on back there?"

Maurice was startled to see the Younguns behind him. "What are you kids doin' here?"

"You ain't leavin' us with no witch!" Terry said.

"You takin' those kids to Speedy's?"

"What else am I goin' to do with 'em?" Maurice asked.

"Them kids will cost extra."

Maurice chuckled. "They always do. They always do."

The Younguns had a great time, calling out to horses, whistling at kids and looking up at the tall buildings. The cabbie shook his head. "You need to get these kids to grow up a bit. They're actin' silly."

Maurice frowned. "Let me tell you a secret, brother. No one ever grows up. They think they do, but their body just gets bigger. Inside, even in you," he said, patting the cabbie on the back, "is a kid who wants to feel free, have a momma and daddy to protect him, and go splash around under a fire hose on Independence Day."

The cabbie smiled, shaking his head. "You're serious, ain't you?"

"Everyone wants kids to hurry and grow up. Become men and women. But you know what?"

"What?"

"There ain't a day goes by that you don't wish you could be a child again. Think about it," Maurice said, then turned. "Hey, kids," Maurice called out. "Look at that big building we're comin' up to."

"What's that?" Terry asked Maurice.

"That's a hospital. You children best hold your breath and don't talk for a while. You don't want to suck in any sick germs, do you?"

The Younguns' eyes went wide and they all sucked in. The cabbie chuckled quietly.

Maurice smiled and sat back, enjoying the sights and sounds—and the silent Younguns who were turning red in the back.

CHAPTER 27

JUKE JOINT JUMPIN'

On the east side of St. Louis, the color line was clearly drawn. The Younguns sat wide-eyed, having never seen so many dark faces in one place at one time.

"Where are we?" Terry asked.

Maurice laughed. "This is the black part of town."

"Why do they all live over here?" Larry asked, looking around at the sights and sounds.

Maurice sighed. "Most of 'em got no choice. Just like at that hotel, some white folks don't seem to want to be near black folks."

"We like you," Sherry said, grabbing Maurice's hand.

He patted her hand. "I know you do. And I loves you all."

"You live near us," Larry said.

"Mansfield's different. Small towns are different. Old money makes people think they's different but when people are 'bout equal with what they have, they don't seem to worry so much 'bout who's white or who's black."

"What's the difference between old money and new money?" Terry asked.

Maurice laughed. "That's just a term for rich and snobby.

Folks that think they's somethin' 'cause some daddy or granddaddy done left them too much money and no manners or common sense."

The cabbie stopped at Speedy's. "Here it is," he said, looking at the gaudy building.

Maurice's eyebrows went up. He leaned over and whispered into the cabbie's ear, "But this is a juke joint!"

"I thought you knew that."

"My cousin Speedy said he ran a rooming house," Maurice said, looking at the people going in and out of the swinging tavern doors. "Never seen no roomin' house that looked like this," Maurice said, shaking his head.

"Looks like a carnival house," Sherry said with a smile.

"Is this where your cousin Speedy lives?" asked Terry.

"I think so," Maurice said, paying the cab fare.

"Why's it look like a saloon?" Larry asked.

"I think 'cause it is," Maurice said, feeling a sinking spell overcoming him.

"What's Pa goin' to say?" Terry asked.

"Lord knows," Maurice said. "Come on, let's go."

As they got off the back of the cab, Larry looked at a couple of very fancily dressed customers coming out of the door. "What does your cousin Speedy do, Mr. Springer?"

"I ain't seen Speedy for years. Last word I got was he was runnin' a boardin' house."

A dandy of a black man looked out the second floor window. "What you want?"

"I'm lookin' for Speedy Springer," Maurice answered.

"Who's doin' the lookin' and why you got three little white kids with you?"

"I'm Speedy's cousin, Maurice Springer, and these are my friends."

"Cousin Maurice!" the man shouted happily. "I'll be right down!"

They heard the sound of clumping feet coming down the stairs and the door flung open. "I'm Speedy! Maurice, how you been?" Speedy shouted, hugging Maurice.

"I'm fine, fine," Maurice said. "We need a place to stay. West Side Hotel won't let a black man in."

"West side of St. Louis is like pickin' cotton in Alabama," Speedy said, pulling back and looking at the Younguns. "And these are your neighbors? Man, you have white neighbors?"

Before Maurice could answer, Speedy pushed them inside. "Come on, come on. There's room at this inn for you all."

Maurice took him aside and whispered. "But this is a juke joint. It ain't a boarding house like I heard you were runnin'."

"Cousin, I tried runnin' a boardin' house, and still let a few rooms to old timers upstairs. But there weren't enough money in it, so the landlord suggested I put in a juke joint to keep up with the rent."

"Sure it's okay for these kids to be here?" Maurice asked.

"I don't want 'em goin' into the bar. But all the cookin' is done on the second floor where the boardin' rooms are. They'll be fine for as long as you need to stay."

"Just a few days, that's all," Maurice said. "Come on, kids. Grab your bags."

As they walked past the entrance, a flashily dressed white couple came out. Speedy shook the man's hand. "Thank you for comin'. Come on back and hear the band we got tonight. They's hot."

"Thanks, Speedy," the man called out. "We'll be back."

Maurice whispered, "You got white customers too?"

"This is the best club in town," Speedy said, winking at his cousin. "Best club in the *whole* town." Terry scrunched his nose at the woman's perfume, but Sherry's eyes lingered on her fine silk dress with ruffles.

Speedy took them to a parlor area and ordered one of the tuxedoed attendants to take the kids to the kitchen and get them something to eat. When they were alone, Speedy smiled, shaking his head. "It's good to see you. How's life down on the farm?"

Maurice brought Speedy up to date while the Younguns looked around. They found the kitchen and were soon eating cake and drinking milk.

In the parlor, Maurice shook his head at Speedy. "You been writin' Eulla Mae all these years 'bout how well you been doin' runnin' a boardin' house. Boardin' house?" he shouted. The band started playing downstairs. "This is a saloon!"

Speedy shrugged. "Cousin, I'm just makin' do with gettin' by. World's hard on a black man tryin' to make somethin' of himself."

"That be so, but you shouldn't be involved with selling liquor."

"Cousin, cousin, this is just—"

Maurice cut him off. "This is just disgraceful. Here I come with children, tellin' 'em that my cousin runs a respectable boardin' house, and come to find that he's runnin' a saloon! Their pa's a minister, what's he goin' to think?"

Speedy shrugged. "What you think is your own business. I'm offerin' you and those kids a place to stay. It just makes good sense for you to stay here."

Maurice shook his head. "I learned a long time ago that they is some good sense you listen to and some you just let go by."

"I ain't forcin' you to go into the bar downstairs," Speedy said defensively.

"Can you help us find another place to stay?" Maurice asked.

"You try the YMCA?"

"They don't take blacks and besides, I got a little girl with me."

Speedy fell silent, then brightened. "I got a friend who owes me a favor down the street. Runs a small hotel, got nice rooms."

"Same kind of place as yours?"

"No, no," Speedy answered. "Just a small hotel, mostly for old people. Good place for you to stay."

"They got rooms you think?"

"I said, he owes me a favor." Speedy stood up. "Let's go get them kids and I'll ride you down to the hotel in my new car."

"Car? You got yourself a car?" Maurice asked, surprised.

Speedy smiled. "Business is booming, it certainly is."

The Younguns had left the kitchen and were wandering through the hallways. When the band started up, they looked around for a way to sneak a peek and found a secret stairway.

Speedy's juke joint was already hopping. Terry peeked through the door at the people crowded around the white-haired piano player with a garter on his sleeve. He was pounding on the keys as fast as he could.

"What kind of music is that?" Terry whispered, wiggling to the music.

"Don't know, but I like it," Larry said, tapping his feet.

"Don't sound like church music," Sherry said.

"Who cares?" Terry said, popping her on the head.

They all fell forward when the door was pulled open. "And who might you be?" said a big woman with her hands on her hips.

"We're visitin' cousin Speedy," Sherry answered.

"Speedy's your cousin?" the woman laughed.

"What kind of music is that man playin'?" Terry asked.

The lady smiled. "Back street juke joint jumpin' music. Come on over and I'll get him to play you a song."

The Younguns trailed closely behind the lady of the house, acutely aware that they had more black people staring at them than they had ever seen before.

At the edge of the stage, the white-haired piano player smiled. "What you kids wanna hear?"

"Somethin' like you were just playin'," Larry said quietly.

"You mean like this?" the man asked, and he let his left hand roam the keyboard in a piano boogie beat.

"Yeah," Larry said, tapping his fingers on the piano. "I like that!"

From throughout the room came shouts of "all right" or "move them fingers."

The piano player added his right hand and soon the whole place was jumpin'. Larry began doing a sort of duck-walk dance around the piano, and Terry shook around like someone possessed. When the piano player finished the song, everyone cheered.

Terry shouted out, "Could you play another?"

Everyone hit the dance floor again as the man's fingers flew up and down the keyboard again. Women were being swung into the air and slid along the dance floor.

Larry danced by Terry and shouted out, "Never knew dancin' could be so much fun!"

Terry did a somersault across the floor and shouted, "This ain't dancin', this is just feelin' good!"

Patrons formed a circle around the Younguns who were doing the strangest looking dances. The big woman whispered to the piano player, "Poor souls, they're *tryin'* to dance."

The piano player grinned.

By the time Maurice and Speedy found the Younguns, the kids were jumpin' and dancin' on top of the piano. Maurice took one look at Sherry on the edge of the piano, shaking all around, and closed his eyes. "Rev. Youngun's goin' to be upset. Man, what am I going to do?"

Speedy laughed. "Why don't you leave and let them stay? Most blacks ain't never had this much fun 'round white folks."

Maurice glared. "They're comin' with me."

Speedy chuckled. "All right, all right. I was just jokin'."

It took him a while to get the Younguns out of the joint because Terry wanted to keep pickin' up the coins being tossed at them for their dancing antics. Once outside, Terry protested. "Why do we got to leave? I love that place."

"'Cause we do," Maurice said, lifting him into the cab. And this place ain't nothin' but trouble for ol' Maurice. You all be quiet now."

Speedy leaned over and whispered, "Nothin' wrong with juke joints. Just another way to make money. Eulla Mae won't never know."

Maurice shook his head. "I'll pray for you, Speedy."

"Good, I probably need some." Speedy smiled and closed the car door.

The hotel Speedy took them to was clean and neat, and the lobby was filled with old people. "I liked the other place better," Sherry said, looking around.

"Yeah," Terry said, "let's go back there. I want to dance some more."

Maurice gathered the children around him. "I want you to forget about goin' to Speedy's. Your pa would never understand."

"You mean fib to Pa?" Larry asked.

"No sir!" Maurice said indignantly. "I'm not askin' you to fib. I'm just sayin' that he won't know to ask if you don't say nothin' 'bout it. That ain't fibbin'."

Terry put his arm around Maurice. "That's my way of thinkin' exactly!"

CHAPTER 28

ANTHROPOLOGY DAY

Alice Roosevelt Longworth telegraphed her father about the disgraceful contests that were being promoted in his name. The president sent a simple message back:

> *Dear Alice:*
> *Use your best judgment. I will stand by you.*
>
> *Father*

Alice made her mind up to do exactly that. *I'll just wait and see what turns out,* she thought. Then she turned her happy thoughts to the dog show and groomed her little dog.

Laura did not sleep well, tossing and turning, going over every word of her conversation with Bambuti. She thought about the wretched life he had led, about his simple dream of seeing his forest again.

"The world looks different through Tao's eyes," she said in the morning.

Manly pulled on his right boot and nodded. "Here some of

them mean folks was callin' him a savage, and the little feller is better than all of 'em put together."

"I wish we could help Bambuti, don't you, Manly?"

Manly nodded. "If he wins, he'll get that prize money and be able to go back home. If he loses, we'll give him some money to help him out."

Laura hugged him. "I'm going to give this to him after the games," she said, showing him the silver locket with her picture in it. "This will get him back home."

"You're givin' him the picture locket I gave you? How's that gonna get him back to Africa?"

"Open it," she said softly.

Manly opened the clasp. Inside was a hundred dollar bill neatly folded and wedged in front of her picture.

"But that's the money you've been savin' for that trip you've always wanted to take to California!"

"I know. But it's the money I've earned from my writing and I want to do it. I want to give it to Bambuti."

"How'll he know how to get back to his forest, wherever it is?"

"Before we leave, we'll write out instructions and help him book his passage home."

Manly thought for a moment, then reached into his pocket and pulled out his emergency fifty-dollar bill from his wallet. "Give him this."

"But that's your—"

"Been savin' it for a life-or-death emergency. Can't think of no better person to give it to than your little friend."

"Oh, Manly."

"Oh, Manly, nothing. It makes me feel good to help out."

After breakfast, they took a cab to the Olympic Game field and walked through the mud to where the Anthropology Day events were being held.

At the stands, Laura and Manly sat quietly, surrounded by

whole families laughing and pointing to the men assembled from around the world. It was like a day at the circus.

Laura waved to Bambuti who smiled and bowed his head. He stood with pride in his simple loin cloth, long used to the laughter of British troops in Africa who tossed coins for him to dance and sing. Tao slipped up and sat beside them.

"Mr. Tao," Laura said, "can't we get Bambuti away from all this?"

"If he wins, he is finally going home," Mr. Tao said. Laura began to pull out the locket, but Manly gently squeezed her hand.

"Not now," he said. "Let's tell him later."

The announcer called for silence. "We're gonna have a fun afternoon, aren't we?" he asked, and the crowd cheered and called for the games to begin.

"Now hold on, hold on. They'll be fallin' all over themselves in a moment. But look behind me," he said pointing to a seventy-five-foot stack of wooden desks, chairs, trees, and lumber, held between a tall, rickety frame. "We're gonna have ourselves a bonfire and Alice Roosevelt Longworth herself, the president's daughter, is here to hand out the prizes. Mrs. Longworth, will you come up here and take a bow?"

Alice Roosevelt Longworth walked onto the small stage and waved to the cheering crowd. She leaned over to the announcer and whispered, "Why aren't you out on the field?"

"What?" he said, leaning back to look into her face.

"You promoters are the real barbarians," she smiled, walking back to her seat.

The announcer walked over to the mayor's aide. "What's gotten into her?"

"You tell me," the aide said. "I can't talk any sense into her."

So the games began. The crowd cheered and laughed, but Laura, Manly, and Tao watched in silence.

On the field, the men climbed poles, jumped over logs, and raced around the track. When any of them stumbled, fell, or hurt themselves running, vaulting, or tossing the hammers, the crowd found great humor in it. And when one competitor knocked himself unconscious against a marker pole, the crowd acted as if it were all part of a vaudeville show.

There was a fifty-foot tree on the edge of the field. Bambuti was one of the men from tribes around the world competing against each other by climbing the tree as quickly as possible. An African from the Congo climbed the tree in thirty-nine seconds. One of the Patagonians climbed it in thirty seconds.

One of the Ainus fell from the tree and broke his wrist while the Moros all climbed it in forty seconds or more. Bambuti was last.

The announcer laughed. "Do you think this little fellow can beat thirty seconds?" The crowd gave the thumbs-down sign.

"Just like the Roman circuses," Tao said quietly.

Bambuti suffered the insults and prepared to climb. When the gun went off, he scurried up the tree in twenty seconds. The announcer was flabbergasted. "Twenty seconds. He climbed faster than any man alive!"

Manly winked. "Score one for Bambuti. He just might win his way home."

"He gets our money no matter what, all right?" Laura asked. Manly nodded.

Bambuti looked toward the stands, wondering what he had done to deserve being brought to the end of the earth. He closed his eyes in silent prayer.

Please give me the strength so that I can go home again. Please don't leave me to die here where I am hated for being born. I want to see the center of the forest again.

As the events dragged on until dark, Laura, sickened by it all, wanted to leave. Then came an announcement: Bambuti would be pitted against three bigger men in a mud fight. The crowd laughed and cheered as Bambuti did his best to fight off his opponents. The winner was the one who was left able to see, and though he fought well, Bambuti was practically blinded from the soft, sticky mud.

The announcer laughed at the three-against-one competition and shouted, "It's bad enough three against one, but this is three against one-half!"

Bambuti, with only partial vision left from his mud covered face, turned away from the crowds. He took a mudball and threw it toward the announcer, hitting him square in the face. The crowd loved it, thinking it was part of the act, until the other men began pelting the crowd with mud.

The announcer screamed out, "Guards! We need some guards out here."

Alice Roosevelt Longworth ran up and grabbed his arm. "You have to end these games. I demand it."

The announcer was under pressure with the events so out of hand and shouted, "You can't demand anything!"

"We'll see," she said, storming off.

It took the police to break up the mud fight and push the men from the field. Bambuti turned again and saw Laura. He raised his fists, bowed his head slightly, then smiled, just as a policeman struck him down with his baton.

Laura stood and grabbed Manly's hand. "He's hurt!"

"Let's get on down there," Manly said, taking her hand. They started forward and Manly turned. "Comin', Mr. Tao?"

"I'm right behind you."

"Watch your step," Manly told him. "These steps are hard to see."

"Watch your step." Mr. Tao smiled. "I've got four eyes, remember?

They pushed their way to where Bambuti was being kept, but the guards at the gate pushed them back. "Can't go in there, lady."

"I'm a reporter and I'm doing a story on one of the athletes."

"Let me see some identification."

Laura showed him her card from *The Mansfield Monitor* and she was allowed through, but they stopped Manly and Tao. "Who're they?" the guard asked.

"They're my assistants. Come on, let them through," Laura said.

"All right, all right. Go on in," the guard said, shaking his head.

Alice Roosevelt Longworth grabbed Jack Dunning's arm and stood him up. "Mr. Dunning, do you have access to a telegraph machine?"

"Yes, back at my office."

"Good," Alice replied. "I want you to send a message to my father."

Dunning paled. "To the president?"

"That's the only father I have," Alice said impatiently. "Now, here's what I want you to send to the White House." Dunning took out his pencil. " 'Father, I am using my best judgment and intend to stop these Anthropology Games.' Just sign it Alice."

"Stop the games?" Dunning said. "Do you know what you're doing?"

"For the first time in a long time I feel good about what I'm doing."

Dunning turned to leave, but she caught his arm. "I want you to add at the bottom, 'P.S. And, Father, you must help the starving people in our cities. They are the ones who really helped elect you. Parts of St. Louis are like an open sore.' "

Dunning ran off to phone the message in. Alice turned to the mayor's aide who had been trying to listen in. "I want you to stop these sick games immediately!"

"I can't do that," he said, feeling faint. "The mayor would fire me."

"And my father will find a way to have the mayor fired if you don't. Well?" she asked.

The mayor's aide opened his collar button and wiped his brow. "I'll see what I can do."

"You just tell them to announce the Anthropology Games over so I can give out the prizes. That's the only way to bring this disaster to a halt."

Ten minutes later, Dunning came running back. "The president . . . er, your father answered!"

"I knew he would," she smiled. She waited a moment, then said, "Well, what did he say?"

"Here," he said, handing her a telegram copy. "He sent it to the Olympic office. This is a copy."

To The Organizers Of The Third Olympics:
I order the Anthropology Games ended immediately.

T. R. Roosevelt
President, United States of America

"Is that all he sent?" Alice asked.

Dunning pulled another telegram from his pocket. "He sent this to you."

Dear Alice:
Games stopped. Is there anything else I can do for you today? I've got a country to run.

Your Father

P.S. I want to help the poor and the starving in America. That is what my fight with Congress is about. They have

closed their eyes to the people who elected me. But I'll keep fighting.

Alice smiled. "That's my father."

Inside the pygmy village, Laura, Manly, and Tao found Bambuti lying on a pile of rags in the corner of the tent. Manly and Tao stood to the side, while Laura knelt down beside him and looked at the cut on his forehead.

Bambuti opened his eyes and smiled. "It is you again."

"I saw you get hit and—"

Bambuti cut her off. "I won't win the contest now." A tear streaked down his muddy face. "I shouldn't have thrown the mud but that man was a devil."

Manly grinned. "Wish there'd been a rock in the mud. You might have knocked some sense into his thick head."

Bambuti focused on Manly. "Who are you?"

Laura blushed. "I'm sorry, I didn't introduce you before. This is my husband, Manly, Manly Wilder."

Bambuti struggled to get up. "I was taught by my second parents to shake hands." He reached out his hand, but dropped it when he saw how mud covered it was.

Manly reached down and shook it anyway. "Mud don't matter. It's a pleasure to shake hands with you."

Bambuti looked up at Tao. "Your feeling was right, Mr. Tao."

Tao bowed. "Perhaps my extra eyes give me extra insight on people."

The guard stuck his head into the tent. "For some reason they've ended the games. You better hurry, 'cause they're about to start the bonfire and give out the medals." He looked at Bambuti. "They want you out there now."

Bambuti stared and the guard shook his head. "I forgot,

you don't speak no English. Well, come on," he said, taking Bambuti's hand.

Laura pressed the locket into Bambuti's other hand and whispered, "Don't worry, you're going home." He gave her a questioning look, but Laura just smiled.

"Come on, pygmy, the announcer's got somethin' special for you," the guard laughed. They watched until Bambuti was out of sight, then took their places back in the stands.

As they sat down, the huge bonfire was lit, and a rush of heat swept over the crowd as the gas-soaked wood ignited. After the cheers of the crowd died down, the announcer began handing out the awards and medals. Alice Roosevelt Longworth watched from the side of the stage, relieved that she had brought the games to a halt.

Though Bambuti had won several of the events, the announcer brought him up on to the stage in his dirty loin cloth to get even for the mud-throwing incident. "And this little man, who don't even know a word of English, this here's the one that threw the mud at me."

The crowd laughed and the announcer nodded. Laura whispered to Manly, "He's going to do something."

"Guards, would you hold him so I can put a mud pie in his face?" Four guards came and gripped Bambuti's arms and legs. The crowds cheered and egged him on as the mud pie was brought on stage.

"Don't let him do this," Alice said to the mayor's aide.

The aide shrugged. "It's only a joke."

"This is not joke. This is sick," she said, watching the four guards struggle to keep Bambuti in place.

Manly stood up. "I'm goin' down. Four against one ain't fair!" He turned to Laura. "I'll make it four against two."

Tao nodded. "I will help. That will make it four against three."

"How about four against four?" Laura said, taking the lead down the stairs.

The crowd was cheering, and the announcer held up his hands. "Course this ain't no ordinary mud pie. This one's a cowpie made special for this little mud-throwing man." Bambuti struggled to get free, but the guards held him tightly.

The announcer called for silence just as Laura stormed onto the stage. "Let him go!" she screamed. Manly and Tao stood at the edge of the stage.

Alice turned to Dunning. "This is getting interesting."

Momentarily caught off guard, the announcer picked the beat back up and smiled. "Well, what have we here?"

Laura walked over and stood next to Bambuti. "This has gone far enough," she said, taking the guards' hands off Bambuti.

"Get her off the stage," the announcer said to the guards.

Alice came up and stood beside Laura. "And as the representative of my father, the president of this country, I order you to keep your hands off her."

The guards looked at the women, and the announcer and didn't know what to do.

The crowd shouted its disapproval at what was happening.

"You all should be ashamed of yourselves!" Laura said to the crowd.

Alice grinned at Laura. "You're doing just fine."

Laura picked up Bambuti's arm and shouted to the crowd, "This is a man, a human being." The crowd began to chatter.

Laura looked at Bambuti and her eyes welled up. She mouthed, *Talk, please talk.*

Bambuti put on the locket and jumped up on the rail. The crowd went silent as he stood before them trembling. "I'm a man. You're white, I'm black, but we both bleed red. We are all God's children. I am one of God's children."

Silent shame swept over the crowd as people gawked at the little man in a loin cloth.

The announcer shook his head, laughed, and cocked back his arm which held the cowpie. "Here's mud in your eye," he said to Bambuti, who stood facing him, without blinking.

"No, in yours," Alice said, and she pushed the cowpie into the announcer's face.

CHAPTER 29

ALICE AND LAURA

It took over an hour for the police to restore order and clear the stands after Alice stopped the games. The promoters tried to evict Laura and have Bambuti arrested, but Alice stepped in and stalled them. Bambuti moved behind Laura. No one noticed Mr. Tao edging up behind them.

"This woman is working on behalf of the President of the United States of America," Alice told the police about Laura.

"She is?" the mayor's aide asked.

"Is that right, lady?" the officer asked Laura.

"She's the president's daughter, she ought to know," Laura said, catching Alice's sly glance.

"But we got instructions to hold this little troublemaker," he said, pointing to where Bambuti had been.

Laura looked around, then saw Mr. Tao walking away. She smiled. There was an extra set of feet under his robe.

"What troublemaker?" Laura asked. "Who on earth are you talking about?"

"He's got to be around here someplace!" the officer said, panicked. "Spread out, everybody. Look for him!"

"Who?" asked one of the workers.

"That midget," said the officer. "He was right here!"

Several of the little people from Tao's exhibit stepped forward from the crowd. "Are you looking for me?" asked the redheaded dwarf.

"Or me?" asked a small Spanish man.

As several others of the little people stepped out, the officer threw up his hands in frustration. "I give up! Come on, men, let's go back to the station."

Manly stood at the edge of the crowd, smiling. Laura saw him and mouthed, "Bambuti?" Manly just nodded and gave her a thumbs-up.

The redheaded dwarf tugged at Laura's skirt. "Mr. Tao said to tell you don't worry about Bambuti. He'll help him get back to Africa."

"Did he say anything else?" Laura asked quietly.

"He said that he was right in his feelings about you, and he thanks you and your husband for the money you gave Bambuti."

Alice walked over. "Is everything all right?" she asked, looking at the little people who had gathered around and then at Laura.

Laura smiled. "Everything couldn't be better."

"We have to go," the redheaded dwarf said.

"Well, good-bye," Laura said, waving to the six men who melted into the crowd.

Alice watched them go, then turned to Laura. "I must say that I'm very impressed with the way you stood up on that stage."

"It was you who saved the day," Laura said.

"Don't be so modest," Alice replied. "My father is the President of the United States, so they wouldn't do anything to harm me. But you . . . that took real courage to do what you did."

"It was just something I felt I had to do."

Alice smiled, shaking her head back and forth. "Have you ever considered a career in politics?"

Laura was caught off guard by the question. "No. Women can't vote and—"

Alice interrupted her with a toss of her hand. "We'll change that soon, don't worry. No, what I meant was have you ever considered leaving Missouri and working in Washington?"

"Washington? You mean the capital?"

"Yes, I could arrange it," Alice smiled. "My father respects women and could use someone like you who speaks up."

"That's very flattering, but I'm happy doing what I'm doing."

"Will you at least consider it?" Alice asked. "You've got a lot to contribute."

Laura smiled. "No, I believe my contribution is through my writing."

Alice paused, staring into Laura's eyes, then said, "I think one day you'll have more impact than you realize."

"I hope so," Laura said.

"I know so," Alice said. She looked at her watch. "Got to go to the dog show. I'll leave the offer open," she said.

Manly walked up and stood by Laura's side. "Might be an offer you should consider," he said half-seriously.

Laura smiled. "And leave you and Rose? Not a chance."

CHAPTER 30

ANOTHER BUGGY RIDE

ev. Youngun and Carla Pobst had been buggy riding for the better part of two hours. They'd stopped twice to walk and hold hands, kissing lightly at the ridge point overlooking the town.

At Willow Creek, away from the eyes of the world, Carla took him in her arms and kissed him. "Oh, Thomas," she sighed, "I wish this moment could go on forever."

"It can," he whispered. "But you have to marry me."

"But it's happening so fast and . . ." she said, stammering.

"I've been thinkin' about it for over a year. I've made up my mind."

"I wish it were just that simple," she said, hugging him tightly.

He stepped back and took out a shiny penny. "I know Willow Creek isn't a wishing well, but make a wish before it sinks to the bottom," he said, tossing the penny over the rail.

Carla closed her eyes and opened them as the penny hit the surface. "I hope it comes true," she smiled.

"What'd you wish?" he asked hopefully.

"If I tell you it won't . . . oh, that's just a silly old wives' tale. I wished that good things happen for both of us."

Rev. Youngun took out another penny and held it up. "My turn," he said, tossing it over the side.

When it hit the surface, she giggled and smiled. "Well, tell me what you wished for?"

He turned and looked into her eyes. "I wished that we were married so we could go home together."

Carla blushed and each reached toward the other, hugging as if they were two survivors. They felt lost in a sea of emotions so strong that it took all their willpower to push away.

"I think we better get back in the buggy," he said, taking her hand.

As they walked back to the buggy, life couldn't have seemed better for Rev. Youngun. He was with the second woman he had loved in his life on a beautiful day in Missouri.

I wonder what the kids are up to now? he thought as he helped Carla into the buggy.

CHAPTER 31

DOGS AND FLEAS

hen they arrived at the dog show, the Younguns were shocked at the reception. Laughing reporters and photographers lined the steps to record the arrival of Dangit, the talking dog.

Maurice was handed a telegram from the P. T. Barnum Corporation, offering to buy Dangit, sight unseen, for five hundred dollars. "Five hundred dollars," Maurice said to the kids, after reading them the telegram. "That's a lot of money. You want to sell him?"

The three kids shook their heads at the same time. Larry said, "Ain't enough money in the world to get us to sell Dangit."

"Yeah," said Sherry, "he's a baluable dog."

Maurice raised his eyebrows and Larry translated. "She means valuable."

"I guess that's right," Maurice said to himself, as he led them to their dog booth. But he thought, *Man, oh man, I'd sell Dangit for five bucks!*

There was so much noise, so much confusion, the Younguns just stared at what was going on around them.

Poodles were being fluffed and primped. Ribbons were being adjusted. Women and men were fawning over their pampered pets as if they were children going for their first recital.

Sherry clung to Maurice, worried about getting lost in the sea of legs, and Larry was embarrassed by the girl in the next booth who winked at him. Terry saw her and looked up at his blushing brother. "You got yourself a real bow-wow slobbering after you."

Maurice noticed and smiled. "She's kind of cute."

"I ain't lookin' at her," Larry said quickly, trying to shake the blush off his face.

Maurice laughed, as the pretty little girl winked again. "Well, she's lookin' at you."

Terry, bored with the waiting, sneaked off to look around. On the next aisle over, he saw a display of glass jars filled with little critters. He looked at the sign above them:

THESE ARE THE ENEMY—FLEAS!

In these jars are an estimated one million fleas. Keep your dogs flea-free with FLEA-AWAY, the safest flea powder on the market

Terry tried to read the sign, but stumbled on some of the words. So he tapped a man who was reading it and got him to explain it.

"There's enough fleas in there to make all St. Louis itch," the man said as he walked away.

Terry peered into the jars, watching thousands of the horrible critters jump, fly, and float in what seemed like clouds of fleas. He felt an involuntary itch come over him and began scratching his back. A woman standing next to him began to itch and soon, a half-dozen others were doing it.

Terry walked away, thinking to himself, *Who'd want to keep fleas in a jar, anyway?* He wandered along, gawking at the strange-looking dogs and silly-looking owners. Then he peeked into the back rooms where cooks, bakers, and waiters were all working on the very elegant formal dinner that followed the contest. It was an annual event, and its tickets were among the most sought-after in St. Louis's annual gala of charity events.

Terry had no idea that all the wealthy women were buzzing about what Alice Roosevelt Longworth had done at the Olympic Games. The only Alice he'd ever heard about was from the *Alice in Wonderland* story his mother once read him.

This was a room full of wealthy people needing to work but never having to. The St. Louis Symphony was setting up around the judges' stage, and florists were floating along, barely touching the ground, working on the hundreds of flower arrangements that lined the room.

The pièce de résistance was a ten-foot-tall ice statue of a poodle. It was surrounded by a hundred flower arrangements and circled by delicate pastries made by French chefs who had come all the way from Paris just for the event. Terry looked at it and shook his head. "That's the biggest icicle I've ever seen," he mumbled to himself.

In another room, chefs prepared a lavish dog dinner for the pets of the wealthy. The dogs were to dine on chopped steak and fresh veal. Just the smell of the expensive meat simmering in the kitchen made Terry hungry.

He needed some air, when he saw the tall open windows on the other side of the room, he thought about the slingshot in his back pocket, and walked over. Along the way, he palmed a handful of hard candy from the dessert line for the wealthy.

Terry sucked on one of the candies and looked for targets out the second floor window. He saw a bird fly by and land on a tree branch in front of him. "Here, birdie," he whispered, putting a piece of the hard candy into the sling. Then he saw them. Below him were a half-dozen beggars and a dozen dirty-faced children with their hands out.

"Don't seem right," Terry said to himself as he put the slingshot away. "Feedin' dogs and not feedin' those kids."

He felt the seventy-five cents in his pocket he'd made from dancing at Speedy's juke joint, and tapped on the window. A girl about his age, dressed in patched rags, looked up. Terry wrapped the coins in a cloth napkin he found on the floor, and dropped it down to the girl.

She opened it hesitantly at first and then brightened when she saw the money. "God bless you, Mister!" she shouted out, racing off down the street to give it to her mother for food.

Terry didn't know what to say, but he felt bad seeing what he'd never seen before.

At their booth, Maurice was nervous. "Where's Terry? I know he's up to somethin'!"

Larry looked around. "He's probably off lookin' at all the dogs."

Maurice panicked, looking around for Terry. *Oh, man, now what do I tell their father? I lost your son. Course that was after he broke a stink bomb on the train and the three of them climbed down bed sheets out of the hotel and hopped a cab. And, oh yes, it was after I took 'em to a juke joint where they danced the boogie woogie in a saloon. You bet I was taking good care of them.*

He felt a tug on his pants leg and looked down. "Where you been?" Maurice asked, picking Terry up. Terry didn't notice the sigh of relief Maurice let out.

"Just walkin' 'round, lookin'."

"And what else?"

Terry shrugged. "Gave some money to a poor girl."

"Oh sure!" Sherry said.

"I did!"

"Fibber!" she shouted.

Terry jumped on her and it took Maurice and Larry to pull them apart. From the front of the room, the band struck up the introduction music. The master of ceremonies, a tuxedo-clad man, waved his arms for silence. "Ladies and gentlemen. Before we begin, I have a rather unpleasant announcement to make."

The crowd hushed as the man unfolded a piece of paper. "The rules committee has declared that we have a potential disqualification situation." A groan was heard throughout the hall, since no one knew who the unlucky entrant was.

"Who is it?" shouted the owner of a poodle.

The speaker held up his hands for silence again. "It seems that someone has made mockery of the contest by claiming to have a talking dog."

Maurice shook his head and looked down at the Younguns. "You monkeys are in big trouble," he said. "Probably gonna put you all in jail."

As people whispered, *There's the talking dog. They're the frauds from Mansfield,* the speaker continued. "The judges have ruled that if it can be proven to our satisfaction that this unnamed-breed dog can talk, then he can stay in the contest. Otherwise, their spot is forfeited and we have declared that Mrs. Sarah Bentley, the sponsor of Mansfield's charity show, will be able to enter her poodle, Rags to Riches, as an honorary entrant."

Sarah Bentley appeared on the stage, waving to the crowd. Her son, Willy, was with her. When he saw the Younguns, he stuck out his tongue.

A small applause was heard from the assembled group of wealthy snobs who knew of Mrs. Bentley. Mrs. Stuyvesant Fish said to the Duchess of Manchester, "She used to be a princess of New York society. But she married for money and landed in a Missouri farm town. Is that a fate worse than death?"

The Duchess whispered back, "No, it'd be worse to marry someone without money." They both giggled behind their fans.

Larry looked to Terry and whispered, "You got your ventrillo?"

Feeling in his pocket, Terry nodded. "Got it."

The speaker shouted, "Will the entrants from Mansfield bring Dangit, the so-called talking dog, up here?"

All eyes were on them now. Maurice said quietly, "Okay, Terry, you got to do your magic now. Ain't no time for cold feet." He pushed them forward, carrying Dangit under his arm. He whispered to the kids, "Just have him say somethin', anythin'. Don't go gettin' lock jaw on me now. I don't want to spend no time in the St. Louie pokey. No sir, don't need to be eatin' no jail food."

The kids didn't say a word, just gulped and walked through the staring, snickering adults. The speaker said to the crowd, "What should we have the dog say? The Gettysburg address? Or should we have him sing 'Meet Me in St. Louis, Louis'?" The whole room broke up with laughter.

At the edge of the stage, Willy sneered at Terry. "My father said that Pocahontas wasn't alive when Custer died, and Geronimo didn't kill him either!"

Terry shrugged. "Then give the arrowhead back along with my dollar back for Dangit's entrance fee."

"You didn't pay nothin'! You owe me a dollar!"

Terry gave him the evil eye. "You either pay me a buck or I'm gonna tell your ma that you cheated her out of a buck."

"You wouldn't."

"Durn sure I will, and nothin's crossed. Not my heart, my arms, my fingers, my toes—or my tongue. You're gonna be in big trouble now."

Maurice reached back and tapped him. "Hush, come on up here and get ready. You know what I'm talkin' 'bout."

Terry looked at Willy. "Give me the buck or I'm tellin' right now."

Silly Willy looked around, then reluctantly pulled a dollar from his pocket and handed it to Terry. "You promised not to tell, remember that?"

"Hope I don't get animalesia," he said, stepping up onto the stage.

"Animalesia?" Willy said, looking very perplexed.

Terry slipped the ventrillo into his mouth and stood my Dangit's side. Larry positioned himself in front, so as to block Terry's mouth as best he could.

The speaker smiled and the crowd hushed. "Well, well, well. So this is the famous talking dog of Mansfield. What's your name, dog?"

Dangit cocked his head and appeared to say, "Dangit, and your breath smells."

The crowd roared with laughter. Mrs. Bentley called out, "I warned you about these little scampsters!"

The speaker, knowing that the crowd could turn against him, put his face close to Dangit's. "I'm gonna ask one more question before we make our decision."

Maurice shook his head and mumbled, "Think your mind's already made up."

The speaker turned. "What'd you say?"

"Nothin, just mindin' my own business."

The announcer looked at Dangit. "What did you eat today?"

Dangit turned his head and the man got closer. The crowd pushed forward, straining to hear. Before Terry could say something Dangit let out a loud belch!

The crowd roared again and Larry shouted out, "He's tellin' you he had salami for breakfast."

"I can tell," the speaker said, fanning his face. "I think we've made our decision," he said, looking at the judges.

Willy sneaked up and slapped Terry on the back, knocking

the ventrillo from his lips. "You're in trouble now," Willy said with a sneer.

Terry reached down for the ventrillo, but Dangit beat him to it and licked it into his mouth. "Give it to me, please, Dangit," Terry pleaded.

Dangit shook his head. The speaker looked at Dangit and started to speak, but Dangit barked with the ventrillo in his mouth so it appeared that the speaker was barking! The whole crowd burst into laughter.

A frilly poodle got loose from its owner's arms, dashed across the stage and nipped at Dangit. Dangit jumped at the poodle and the two ran off the stage howling. Larry ran after his dog, followed by Sherry and Terry.

The speaker screamed, "Call the police! Arrest that dog!"

Maurice sighed. "Pokey here I come."

The Younguns tried to catch Dangit, who nipped at the screaming poodle. Maurice took off after them, hoping to get them out the back door before they caused any more trouble.

Two policemen came running through the doors, blowing their whistles. Dangit saw them and made a hard left turn to avoid being caught. He ran under tables, knocking over owners who unleashed their dogs, and soon it was utter chaos.

Dangit ran into the kitchen, jumped onto a long baker's table, and ran through the cakes. Larry was on his trail and shouted, "Dangit's doin' the cake walk!"

At the end of the table, Dangit jumped into a five-foot bin of flour and jumped out again, totally white. Sherry laughed. "Looks like a snowman."

Waiters, oblivious to what was going on in the show hall, carried trays of food toward the dining area. Dangit ran between their legs, knocking them down like bowling pins.

Willy came running into the kitchen shouting, "I told my momma on you!"

Terry picked up a cake and walked over to Willy and smiled.

"Got somethin' for you," he said, then rubbed it in Willy's face.

Dangit pushed his way through the dining room doors and ran down the tables of the wealthy patrons who had retreated from the chaos into their privileged sanctuary.

He ran toward the ice statue and jumped against it. The ice-dog statue teetered back and forth. Maurice came in to the room and walked back out again, saying, "I don't want to see it. What I don't know 'bout, the police can't ask me 'bout."

The ice statue crashed, making a terrible, slippery mess. Dangit made a quick exit, and ran back into the dog show hall, knocking over owners and unleashing more dogs.

Terry rolled the broken ice head along the floor like a bowling ball, knocking over a line of waiters who carried bowls of tomato gelatin and split pea soup.

Two policemen stood in the aisle, blowing their whistles for Dangit to stop, but Dangit barreled straight toward them. Sherry looked up and saw a dogcatcher in a white suit with a big net come racing into the hall. "Look, Terry, the dog catcher's here!"

"We're in trouble now fursure," Larry said. "Come on, we got to get Dangit before they catch him."

Terry, always quick with an angle, shouted to the policemen, "Watch out! He's a mad dog! Mad dog comin' at you!"

The policemen backed away as Dangit came near them. "Keep that mad dog away from me," one policeman shouted as he backed straight into the flea display.

As the flea-filled jars teetered, Terry grabbed Larry's arm. "We gotta get out of here!"

Maurice grabbed up all three of them. He put Larry on his back and Sherry and Terry under his arms, and carried them off toward the exit. "What 'bout Dangit?" Sherry cried.

"Can't worry 'bout him now," Maurice shouted. "We got to get outta here 'fore the police catch *us.*"

From behind them they heard the crash of glass. Maurice stopped. "What was that?"

"That," Terry said looking back at the broken flea jars, "was all heck breakin' loose."

"What you mean?" Maurice asked.

"Someone just knocked over those jars that had . . . a million fleas in 'em."

Suddenly, everyone around the broken jars began to scratch. Dogs howled, nipping at their bellies. Then it spread throughout the room.

"Fleas, million of fleas!" screamed a flea-covered man who raced past them and jumped into the horse trough at the bottom of the stairs.

"Time to flee," Terry shouted, beginning to itch.

Maurice saw that policemen were blocking the exits, so he ran to the fire escape window and put the kids down. He opened the window and pointed out. "Climb out and let's get outta here."

One of the policemen came racing up, itching as he ran. "There's the owners of the dog. Stop 'em!"

Maurice pushed Sherry and Terry out. Larry followed closely behind. Maurice looked around and saw the mass chaos. Sarah Bentley ran by screaming, her face covered with fleas. "Prison here we come," he sighed, then climbed out the window.

The policeman shouted through the window. "Come back! Stop, come back!"

Terry shouted back, "Can't hear you. Got wax in my ears."

Maurice laughed. "Yeah, me too."

At the bottom of the fire escape, Larry swung down on the weighted ladder and rode it to the ground. He held it in place as the others came down.

"I won't leave without Dangit," Larry said.

"There he is!" Terry shouted, pointing up.

Dangit was on the second floor fire escape, barking for them to wait.

"Here, boy, come here, boy," Larry called out.

Dangit looked around, then prepared to jump. The dog-catcher stuck his big net out and caught Dangit in mid-air.

"He got Dangit," Sherry whispered.

Terry moaned. "You got to save him, Mr. Springer. Dog-catcher will kill him fursure."

"What are we gonna do?" Larry said, groaning.

"I don't know," Maurice said, shaking her head.

Alice Roosevelt Longworth, who arrived at the dog show late because of the controversy at the games, stuck her head out the window screaming, "My dog! Has anyone seen my little black dog?"

"That's the president's daughter!" a man shouted.

The door banged open a little way down the alley, and the dogcatcher came out carrying Dangit in his net. He opened the cage on the back of his truck and put Dangit inside.

A little black dog with a sparkly collar, jumped out, but the dog catcher caught him and threw him back in the cage. "That's her dog," Larry said.

"Whose dog?" Maurice said, trying to figure out what to do.

"Alice's. That's the president's daughter's dog that she got from the Empress of China. I saw a picture in the newspaper."

The dogcatcher started his truck and backed up slowly. Dangit howled and the other five dogs inside wailed along with him.

"Come on! We got to save Dangit!" Larry shouted, racing down the alley.

Terry and Sherry followed behind, leaving Maurice alone. "Now they're gonna add breakin' into the dog catcher's truck to their list of charges," he said.

He followed behind them and as the truck went around the corner, he saw the Younguns holding on to the back. "Lord, have mercy on me. Please get us home, Lord. I'll never go nowhere, do nothin' with them again. Please."

Larry tried to undo the latch, but Dangit kept licking his fingers though the cage. "Quit it, boy."

"Larry, I'm fallin'," Sherry cried out. Larry turned and pulled her back onto the truck.

Terry said, "I can open the cage." With a quick turn, he opened the door. The truck took a sharp turn and knocked Terry backward.

"Help!" he called out.

Larry turned and saw Terry holding onto the cage door, which was hanging out over the edge of the truck. Then he saw a parked truck ahead and pulled Terry back in.

The dogcatcher turned around and blinked. "What are you kids doing back there?" he shouted, stopping the truck.

"We're savin' the president's daughter's dog," Larry said.

Terry winked at his brother and whispered, "Now you're thinkin' like me."

"Alice Roosevelt's dog? What are you talkin' about?"

Larry reached in and pulled the small, black dog with the shiny collar out of the cage. "You better take this dog back to her or you're gonna lose your job!"

Dangit jumped into Larry's lap and begain licking him all over. "Put that dog back!" the dogcatcher shouted.

"He's our reward," Larry said with a grin, pushing Dangit away.

"Reward?" asked the dogcatcher.

"Yeah, for findin' Alice Roosevelt's dog and savin' your job."

The dogcatcher spun the truck around and raced back. As he came to a stop, the Younguns jumped off. Alice was standing on the stairs. "My dog! You found my dog!"

Larry handed it to her and smiled. "Give my regards to the president, okay?"

Maurice came up and herded the children and Dangit away.

"Thank you Miss President . . . er, I mean Mrs. Alice. We, ah, got to go."

Two policemen came running from the doors, their faces covered with flea bites. "Those are the kids! Stop 'em!"

"Guess we don't get the thousand bucks," Terry shouted, running behind Sherry, Larry, and Maurice. Alice watched them race away.

"Let's just hope that we get out of here before they figure out who we are!" Maurice said.

He flagged down a cab and pushed them in. "Are they gonna call the Texas Rangers after us?" Sherry asked, hiding under Maurice's arm.

"I hope not." Maurice closed his eyes then looked toward heaven. *Lord, I ain't never goin' nowhere with the Younguns again. You can mark my words, I ain't never goin' no place, not even across the street with them, if you'll just let me get back to Mansfield.*

"Who were those kids?" Alice asked Jack Dunning.

"Some minister's kids, the Younguns. They claimed to have a talking dog, but they got tossed out of the contest."

"So they didn't win?" she asked, petting her dog.

"Nope, they didn't win the prize money."

"I'll have to do something about that," she said.

CHAPTER 32

BACK TO MANSFIELD

Rev. Youngun held Carla's hand as they stood at the train station. "I'll miss you," he whispered. "I want you to come back and—"

She cut him off. "Remember. No promises for now. I'll be back and we'll see how our relationship goes."

He nodded. "I guess you're right."

"And on my next trip, I want to spend time with your children."

Hope that won't be your last trip, he thought. "That would be great. I know they're looking forward to really spending some time with you."

The train pulled away, and Rev. Youngun watched it until it was out of sight on its way to Cape Girardeau. He stood there deep in thought until the train from St. Louis arrived with his children on board.

The kids jumped off and flew into his arms. "Pa! Pa! We missed you!" Terry shouted.

He laughed and hugged them. "How was the dog show? Anything excitin' happen?"

Larry shrugged. "Nothin' much. Just a bunch of dogs, that's all."

Rev. Youngun looked around. "Where's Maurice?"

"I'm right here," Maurice said as he struggled to get off the train with Dangit in the crate.

"Were the children good?" he asked.

Maurice looked at the six eyes staring up at him and sighed. The three Younguns sighed along with him, hanging on the silence of anticipation. "Well," he said, "they were regular . . . angels. We had a good time. Why, we heard some music, took a cab tour of the town, stayed at a fine hotel, saw a high society dance, and then went to the dog show."

"Dangit didn't win, did he?" Rev. Youngun said, looking down at the dog.

"No, Dangit didn't win," Maurice said, reaching down and letting Dangit out of his box. "But he certainly did put on a show," Maurice said, winking at the children.

"He sure did, Pa!" Terry said, knowing they were out of the woods this time.

"So he tried his best but didn't win, is that right?" Rev. Youngun asked, patting Dangit on the head.

"Oh, he put on a good show, yes he did," Maurice nodded. "Had everybody jumpin' round over his act."

Rev. Youngun grinned. "I hope this has been a lesson to you that you can't use tricks or gimmicks to win contests."

"You're right, Pa," the Younguns answered.

"And you have to always compete fair and square. Funny business will just get you in trouble."

"We don't like funny business. No way!" Terry shouted.

Rev. Youngun looked at his red-haired son. "Terry, I think you believe it, don't you?"

"Yes, Pa."

When their father turned, the three Younguns just rolled their eyes. He shook Maurice's hand. "I'm glad you were able to go. I know it meant a whole lot to them. Come on, kids. Let's get home."

"Hey, Terry, I want my dollar back!" Terry turned to see a swollen-faced Willy Bentley standing on the train steps.

"What happened to you?" Rev. Youngun asked, grimacing at all the bite marks on Willy's face.

Maurice pulled on his arm. "Come on, Reverend, it's time we got goin'."

Sarah Bentley appeared behind her son. Her face was also a mass of swollen bites. She was carrying her dog, Rags to Riches, whose eyes were swollen shut.

Larry took his father's other arm. "Let's go, Pa."

When they got to the wagon, Rev. Youngun asked Maurice, "Why were their faces all swollen?"

Maurice looked at the Younguns. "Guess maybe they're allergic to fleas or somethin'," he said.

Rev. Youngun pulled the wagon forward, never hearing the collective sigh of relief behind him. As they rode off he said to them all, "I want you to tell me all about the trip. It sounds like Maurice watched you all very carefully and that you all were good children."

The Younguns nodded from the back of the wagon, crossing their arms, fingers, legs, ankles, and toes. Maurice turned around and mouthed, *You owe me.*

Laura and Manly got off the special train car with private rooms. "Manly, that was a wonderful idea. I never imagined we'd ride back in our own private pullman room. I still don't know how you arranged it."

"Don't ever take me for granted, Laura. I'm just full of surprises." Manly grinned at her and kissed her cheeks. "As far as I'm concerned, we're still on our honeymoon."

Laura blushed and took out the bear Manly won for her. "I think I'll just hug my Manly Bear tonight."

Over the next few weeks, life settled back to normal in Mansfield. Laura received a commendation from President Roosevelt for helping to stop the disgraceful games and Manly had it framed for their parlor wall.

Alice Roosevelt Longworth sent each of the Younguns a ten dollar bill as a reward for finding her dog. They immediately took their money to Maurice to ask what they should do with it. Maurice convinced them to put the money in the church poor box. "It's better than tryin' to explain to your Pa how you earned the money in the first place," he told them.

Half a world away, Bambuti stopped at the edge of the Ituri Forest. With the money that Laura and Manly had given him, he'd come back to Africa by boat, landing in Zanzibar. He rode on the back of a wagon to Stanleyville, then walked the rest of the way home. At the trading post, he wrote a postcard to Laura, sending it by way of Mr. Tao.

For Bambuti, the rest of the way was very emotional. Every step was a memory of something from the images of a little boy's mind. His parents hugging him, teaching him to hunt, and about the ways of the people.

The Ituri Forest. He'd not seen it since his capture on his fifth birthday. But he could feel it inside—inside his soul.

After a two-hour walk, he felt the eyes of people watching him. Then, from out of nowhere, a fellow pygmy with a bow and arrow stepped out.

"What do you want?" the little man asked, in their native language.

"And who are you?" Bambuti asked, remembering the tongue he had been taught by his parents.

"I am Afilobo. I asked you, what do you want?"

"I want to come home."

"Who are you? You are little, but you do not dress as we do."

"I am Bambuti, grandson of Bambuti Matuneo, whom I am named after."

Without saying a word, Afilobo touched Bambuti. Then he said, "Your family is sung about in legends, about the capture by Stanley, and how he took you to the heavens."

"Is my grandfather alive?"

Afilobo sighed. "He is waiting for the butterflies of the forest to take him to God."

"Please take me to him."

They passed a woman carrying a freshly killed monkey and then a group of children playing near the first hut at the edge of the village. At an aging hut, Afilobo pointed inside. "There lies your grandfather. Go to him."

Bambuti entered in silence. His grandfather, frail and white-haired, lay on an animal skin, tended by an elderly woman. "Grandfather. It is I, Bambuti. I have come home."

Tears came to the old man's eyes. "I hoped you would someday come back. But now the end of my time is at hand. I want to see the center of the forest before I die. Take me."

Bambuti lowered his head. "I can't remember the way."

His grandfather lifted his chin. "You carry me and I will show you the way to the center of the forest."

The villagers lined the way to the edge of the gathering of huts, silently watching the old man make his final visit. Bambuti walked in silence, following the grunts and finger-pointing of his grandfather. They walked deeper into the forest, crossed creeks, and inched across fallen trees over raging rivers, through secret passages and ravines.

They followed a curving river, pushed through thick foliage at the bend, and stopped. "It is the most beautiful place I have ever seen," Bambuti said, as thousands of butterflies swarmed around them.

He carried his grandfather through the clouds of dancing butterflies, stepping over flowers that carpeted the forest floor. At the edge of the water, Bambuti's grandfather pointed to a small island in the center that seemed alive with butterflies and flowers. "That is the center of the forest."

Tears flowed down Bambuti's cheeks. He was home, in the center of the forest. He opened the silver locket that hung around his neck and looked at the picture of Laura. "Thank you," he whispered, "for helping me to come home."

Laura worried about whether Bambuti had made it back to Africa, back to the center of the forest. "Do you think he's all right?" she asked Manly every evening before they said goodnight.

"Let's hope so." Manly told her.

Then the postcard came. A postcard all the way from Africa. It had been sent to Laura by way of Mr. Tao. Bambuti had written only three words, but for Laura and Manly, they were more than enough.

I made it.

Laura ran from the mail box, shouting for Manly. "He made it! Bambuti made it!"

Manly hugged her, then looked at the card.

"Did you see this?" Manly asked, pointing to the bottom of the card where a line was written in tiny penmanship.

Laura took the card and read, *"My feeling about you was right. Mr. Tao."*

"I could have told him that," Manly said, hugging her.

"Oh, Manly, this is the best honeymoon present anyone could have given me." Laura smiled and hugged the card.

Later that evening, Laura wrote in her diary:

Some things are truly worth waiting for. Like my honeymoon. I think that taking it almost twenty years after our marriage gave us the chance to renew our vows and truly appreciate the love we have for each other.

I also received a gift of understanding. I had the opportunity to view life through Mr. Tao's strange eyes and walk in the small footsteps of Bambuti. Neither of them could be more different from me. Yet we are the same . . . which I will always remember. It is a gift I will try to pass on to everyone who will listen.

For Laura, it was another small but important lesson learned. She had again touched the lives of people around her in a way that would last forever.

ABOUT THE AUTHOR

Thomas L. Tedrow is a bestselling author, screenwriter, and film producer. His books include the eight-book "Days of Laura Ingalls Wilder Series": *Missouri Homestead, Children of Promise, Good Neighbors, Home to the Prairie, The World's Fair, Mountain Miracle, The Great Debate,* and *Land of Promise,* which are the basis of a new television series. His eight-book series, "The Younguns," to be released in 1993, has also been sold as a television series. His first bestseller, *Death At Chappaquiddick,* has been made into a feature film. He lives with his wife, Carla, and their four children in Winter Park, Florida.